Living with a Cheetah
...or More

Orange Hat Publishing
www.orangehatpublishing.com - Waukesha, WI

www.orangehatpublishing.com
Waukesha, WI

I would like to dedicate this book to my family, friends, fans of reading, the Pfister family, future fans, and especially the Waukesha North Class of 2004 who made the original a big hit.

Acknowledgment

I would like to take time to say a special thank you to those who have made this book what it is today. I would like to give thanks first and foremost to God for implanting this gift in me and giving me the ability to share with you a wonderful thing He has created. I could not have done this without Him.

To my family for the love, prayers, and support through this long process. To my brother, Ben, who gave me the inspiration and reminded me of my love for reading by giving me a book as a gift. To my friends, co-workers, church friends, Waukesha North Alumni, and Facebook friends for checking in with me and keeping me focused on the finished line. To my future fans, may this be a starting block for the rest that is to come and may we all enjoy the ride that we are going to take together. To Tammy Jo, for giving me a reason not to settle for anything less of who I am and believing in me that I do have potential in life.

To Kathie Giorgio, Dasha Kelly, Patricia Skalka, Ally Condie, and Dr. Amanda DeSua for inspiring me to keep writing with the words you have written and shared. I hope to be an inspiration to others as you have been to me. To the All Writers Workshop family, for helping me finish a work in progress that looked like a disaster. To my writing coach, Summer Hanford, for helping me polish my work, being a helpful friend, giving me a clear insight into the world of writing, and giving me encouragement only a writing coach could give.

To the Orange Hat Publishing family for helping me get my book out into the world, making its presence known, and especially giving my book an identity. The cover looks great; I am still in awe of it. To my editor, Christina Schuler, for helping me dot the "I's" and cross the "T's." Your thoughts and comments are implanted in this book and I appreciate all you have done to help me get to the finish line. And last but not least, to Shannon Ishizaki, words cannot express what you have done for me and I really appreciate you giving a young writer the opportunity to be able to share his words with the world and presenting the stepping stones to a wonderful path and journey that could hopefully lead to my dream job. I thank God for your faith in my writing and believing in me. I will never forget our phone conversation about how you thought the book was sort of bizarre and remembered that there is an audience that enjoys reading bizarre things. I am grateful that you gave my story a chance when others flat out said no. My heart is touched deeply with all the work you put into this book. Please know your work has not gone unnoticed.

Living with a Cheetah ...or More

by Michael Young

Orange Hat Publishing
www.orangehatpublishing.com - Waukesha, WI

Day One

It's said everything happens for a reason. The reason for that is . . . I don't know, but I'm sure there is one. If I were honest with you, I would say the reason is for us, as humans, to change or grow. As I look back at my once-enjoyable life, I would say to you that I wouldn't have changed a single thing about it for anything. Well, there may be one thing I would change.

It all started a while back. I was working on my dairy farm in Cowlic, Arizona at the time. The farm had been in my family for many generations. It used to be bigger than it was now, but due to not enough help and most of the farm being sold to the government it became a hobby farm for me. I loved working and doing things around the farm so much that I never found much time to go to college or find a dream job. For me, farming was all I knew.

To get to the farm, you would have to take I-10 west to Highway 86. That will take you to Sells, where you'll head southwest toward Cowlic. Cowlic is in Pima county and my farm is thirty miles north of downtown Cowlic. It takes a while to get there due to a lot of hills on the way. Once you see the barn, there is a dirt driveway that leads to an average two-story house.

The first floor has a kitchen, bathroom, den, and living room. There are two staircases in the house. One goes up to the second floor and the other down to the basement. In the basement, I do my laundry and have a workshop. Up the main flight of stairs are a hallway and two doors. One of the doors leads to another bathroom and the other leads to my bedroom.

Outside the house is a dirt path that takes you to two barns. Next to the house are a bunch of calf hutches where the calves live. To the right of them is a bunny house. There is a small fence around it so the bunnies don't run away. Next to that are two dog houses. The first house belongs to a German shepherd named Duke. Duke is a very good watchdog. The other dog is Taz. Taz is a Rottweiler who loves to run around the yard and fetch his ball.

The Rottweiler is my favorite dog. It's hard for me to describe why I like Taz a lot, but I do. I like how Taz's face looks when he sees you, with or without his tongue hanging out. It doesn't matter to me. He looks even cuter with his ears pricked up.

I usually unhook the dogs from their chains and let them play around for a while. Dogs need time to run around and get their exercise so they can stay active. After about thirty minutes of play time, I hook them back up to their chains. Then, I continue toward the first barn, which is on the left side of yard. The first barn holds all the Jersey cows and the second, to the right, holds Holstein cows.

Living in Arizona is a treat. It's warm most of the year. The average high is about 80 degrees and the average low is around 50. In the morning, you can smell the dew from the night air. When the wind blows, it makes the stalks of grain, blades of grass and leaves on the trees dance freely. When it rains, the plants delight in each drop, quenching their thirst. The best thing about Arizona is the sunsets. When the sun goes down, the sky turns from a bright blue ocean into a majestic rainbow. You can see all the colors in the sky during this time. It is an astounding, breath-taking phenomenon. To live in Arizona is truly a blessing from God.

One morning in May while I was reading the paper, I noticed through one of the kitchen windows that the sky was red. In Arizona, the sky is never red, even on a Monday. As I sat in the kitchen drinking my coffee and reading my paper, I came upon an article talking about the weather. It seemed that places all around the U.S. were experiencing crazy weather phenomenons. I couldn't believe what I was reading. The author pointed out that it had been raining in New York for the past five days and wasn't letting up. In Los Angeles, they had witnessed five tornados within two miles of each other. *Oh, my.* Texas was seeing snow fall from the sky and Florida had sub-zero temperatures. It was hard to understand what was going on in the world. I just kept wondering how the sky could go from the dark black of night to bloody red. Once I finished pondering this crazy phenomenon, I got up and went over to the sink to wash out my cup.

As I made my way toward the Jersey barn to let the cows out, I heard the sound of something rumble along the gravel driveway. The noise came from the tires of a big black hummer. I tried not to panic as the vehicle got closer to me. I was a little confused why it was here. In Arizona, you don't see a lot of hummers, especially in the country. When you see one, it usually means official business. The massive vehicle stopped in front of me. As the dust from the gravel settled, I took a deep breath. Both front doors opened up. Out came two big guys dressed in black secret service uniforms and wearing sun glasses. They looked like two big linebackers you'd never want to face on a football field. They both adjusted their ties and just looked at me. After a while, they closed their doors and started to walk toward me.

The first guy was white with blond hair cut into a flattop. The other guy was black, like me. He had black hair, cut very short. His face had a very familiar look on it, as if I knew who he was. I was bewildered and puzzled where I had seen his face before. The white man's nametag said *Agent Smithers*, and the other guy's said *Agent Thompson*.

Agent Smithers asked me, "Are you Mr. Ellington?"

"Yes," I answered.

My name is James Ellington. I grew up during the Civil Rights Movement. In fact, I was a witness to some of the events that took place during that time. No, I am not related to Duke Ellington, but I have met him. I saw him at a café in Sells once. We were both at the counter and, while we had lunch, I talked to him about life as a farmer and he shared some stories of the road life of a musician. I was involved with the Freedom Riders and sit-ins during the Civil Rights Movement. I don't have a wife or any children because I never met anyone who would want to spend the rest of their life on a farm. Being the oldest of my siblings, my parents didn't want me to go to college. They wanted me to be able to take care of the farm once they left.

My parents, Charles and Marie, died in a plane crash when I was about thirty and that's when I took over the farm. My sister Ruth, who is now sixty years old, and my brother John, who is sixty-five, are what's left of my family. Ruth lives in Manhattan, with her husband James and two girls. John lives in sunny San Francisco, with his wife Starla and two boys. Ruth and John keep in touch by writing me letters every now and then. I also get Christmas cards from them each year. They send the cards where you can put a family photo on it so I can see how grownup they all are.

Agent Thompson brought my thoughts back to reality, saying, "We have a letter from the President for you." He held it out.

"What letter?"

Agent Thompson held out a business sized envelope. The letter read:

Mr. Ellington,

This is a very unusual request. The government and I have been discussing an experiment we think would be very beneficial for science. Our experiment consists of a human trying to tame a wild animal in a domestic environment. The hope is to have a closer interaction between the two species. After several studies and much consideration, it was determined that Arizona would be a prime location and that you and your farm would be ideal for the experiment. Your country would be indebted to you for your participation.

You will receive compensation for doing this experiment. First, you will get all the necessities you will need for the animal. The items will be shipped to you. Second, for participating in the experiment, you will no longer have to pay annual taxes. The animal that will be sent to you is a cheetah. Your consideration is greatly appreciated. Please let the gentlemen who gave you this letter know your response. Thank you for your time.

Sincerely,

Leo L. Schmidt,

President of the United States

I couldn't believe my eyes. Did that last part say the animal was a cheetah? *A cheetah??* How could this be? The government and President chose one of the world's most dangerous animals. Why couldn't it have been a grizzly bear, or Siberian tiger, or maybe an African elephant? This must have been part of their discussion. I still could not figure out why they wanted me and why it was a cheetah. The thought of a cheetah on a farm was not something a farmer dreamed about at night. Maybe a child living on a farm would. I debated back and forth in my head. I tried listing pros and cons about the situation. Every time I thought of a response, some other variable would enter my mind and I would have to start all over. I stood hunched over, trying to think if I could make it happen, but nothing seemed to work.

The next thing I was aware of during my contemplation was Agent Thompson handing me a contract to sign. I wasn't aware that I had made my decision yet. Agent Thompson reached in his pocket for a pen. As the pen came out, I realized where I'd seen his face before.

When I was in my twenties, I worked for a man named Mr. Dubois, in Winchester, Arizona, who really hated blacks. He took on a little black boy named Sam to help out around the house. Now, Mr. Dubois had a natural tendency to drink a lot and take his frustrations out on his help, as we were still treated like slaves back then. One day, I was working in the yard when Mr. Dubois got home. No matter what mood Mr. Dubois was in during the day, when he got home from drinking, he would look for Sam and would teach Sam "some respect." Mr. Dubois' way of getting respect was whipping Sam, and tying Sam's hands together and letting him hang from a tree for hours. I felt bad for Sam. It wasn't his fault he was black, and you shouldn't beat up someone just because they're different from you. I told Mrs. Dubois what was going on and she was furious. She yelled at Mr. Dubois for what he had been doing to Sam. Two days later, Mrs. Dubois took Sam away from Mr. Dubois for good. I was happy to know Sam wouldn't have to take any more abuse from Mr. Dubois, and I felt proud of what I'd done. After that, I was fired and went to live on the farm with my family.

Looking at Agent Thompson, I realized he was Sam. I was touched to know that something positive came out of helping a little boy from Winchester. I knew then and there that I needed to sign the contract and see if there was something I could possibly do to help mankind out. I handed the contract back to him with a grin.

At that moment, a vision came to me. I saw a picture in my head of myself standing in a field where the cheetah was living. The cheetah saw me and started to run toward me. Duke and Taz stood next to me, barking. As the cheetah got closer, the vision started to spin and I got dizzy.

"Mr. Ellington," Agent Smithers asked. "Are you okay?"

"Oh, I'm sorry. I'm still a bit tired from going to bed late last night and at age seventy-two that is no joke."

"We need to get back and start processing the paperwork. Take it easy and we hope it works out for you. Goodbye."

"Yes, enjoy the rest of your day, gentlemen," I said.

They got in the hummer and backed down the driveway. I tried to take it all in. A few minutes went by before I realized I had work to do. I always did my chores before I could get on with my day.

My day usually starts with me heading to the barns and milking all the cows. When that is done, I take them out of their stalls and lead them out to roam in the field. Once all the cows are out of the barns, I clean the stalls and get them ready by filling their mangers with hay and the troughs with water. When the barns are finished, I take care of the rabbits, dogs, and calves, and clean their houses as well. After I complete my chores, I get to enjoy most of the day to myself before I bring the cows back into their barns and milk them again at night.

Every month, a veterinarian comes to check on the animals. I will usually greet him and see how he's doing. Then we both head out to check and see how each animal is doing and what they need. My neighbor, Ted, is a hay farmer. Because I don't have time to produce hay, he and I agreed for him to give me some of his hay for some of my milk. It's nice to have neighbors in a community helping each other out.

After I got my chores done and made my way back to the house, I noticed the sky changed from red to blue. When I got to the house, I decided to have a nice lunch. I made a turkey sandwich with lettuce, tomato and cheese. A slice of pickle and sea salt chips accompanied the sandwich. I poured a glass of premixed raspberry and peach iced tea. This is one of the best drinks ever made. I grabbed everything and headed into the living room.

In my living room, I have a chair with a little standing tray to put my cup and plate on while I watch TV. About five feet from the chair is an entertainment stand with a television and VCR on it. I have a bunch of books and VHS movies. They're on a long bookshelf to the left of the entertainment stand. The books and movies are all Christmas presents from my family. I know of some Amish farmers that go through life without television and all sorts of other electric appliances, but my family wanted me to have something to do besides my daily chores.

I turned the television on. Upon finishing my lunch, I went back to the kitchen and refilled my cup. As I returned to my chair, I stopped at the bookshelf. I looked for a certain book to get some information before the cheetah arrived. I knew the cheetah wouldn't get here tomorrow, but I thought it was a good idea to know what I was getting into before I had no idea what to do. The book on my shelf was called *Cheetah: The Spotted Feline*. I received this book from my sister, because when I was younger, my favorite animal was the cheetah, and she thought it was a good idea to get a book all about cheetahs. I grabbed the book and went back to my chair. I started to page through the book and found some interesting facts. Fifteen minutes later, I set the book on a tray, and decided to take a nap.

I had a dream while I was napping. In my dream, I was in the field where the cows roam. The sky was brownish red in color and the ground was brown with weeds. The barns were torn apart in places, as if a tornado went through and destroyed them. The fence that kept the cows from running away looked old and rusty. The paint was eroding off of everything. I couldn't believe what had happened to the farm. It looked like a vast number of bugs with help from the weather destroyed it. As I walked, I tried to find the animals. I noticed a big kettle in the field, where the land looked like it had a big hole in the ground, like an asteroid hit. In it I saw a huge pile of animal carcasses. I walked down into the kettle to get a closer look. The dead animal bodies were giving off a potent smell so powerful; I had to cover my mouth and nose. I reached for a skull and picked it up. It resembled the head of a Jersey bull. It was then that I realized that *all* the bones were from cows. It was a pit full of dead cows, all of which had been eaten and left there. My face started to tense up and I could feel this rage build stronger inside of me as I looked at the pile of carcasses. I threw down the skull and stormed out of the kettle. Once I reached the top, I scanned the rest of the field. Finally, I came full circle and saw the cheetah in the distance. As I approached him, he was crouched low to the ground. I stopped at one point and heard a voice in my mind. *The cheetah lies low to the ground when it gets ready for an attack.* That sounded so familiar. I tried remembering where I heard that before. *Ah-ha!* I thought. That was one of the facts in the book I read. After the word *attack* went through my mind, the cheetah got up from the ground and started to sprint toward me, with its pace quickening as it came closer. I just stood there. The cheetah jumped into the air and I stuck my hand out to try to stop it. As the cheetah was about to collide with me, I woke up from my nap. I was sweating and gasping for air. My heart was pounding so hard, I could feel it trying to jump out from my chest. The dream felt so real to me. I tried to pull myself together and figure out where I was. The sun was still out and it was still afternoon. I went outside to get some fresh air.

Day Fifteen

Two weeks later, I was in the kitchen and heard the dogs barking outside. I walked to the front door to see what caused the commotion. There was a big B.I.G. truck in the drive way. B.I.G. is a company that delivers packages and parcels across the country. They might deliver across the globe as well.

The driver poked out his head and asked, "Are you Mr. Ellington?"

"Who the heck are you?"

"I have a bunch of packages for you that were sent by the President," said the driver.

"Well now, just out of curiosity, how many are there?" I asked.

"Oh, you have about twenty-five," he said after looking through his sheets. "The President ordered them a while back and had us wait till a gentleman called saying we could make the delivery." The driver got out of the truck and walked toward me with his package scanner device. He handed it to me to sign saying I received the delivery. Next, he got a dolly from the side of the truck to put packages on. Five packages went to the side of the barn and the others went into the house. Once he finished, he put his dolly away and closed the back of his truck. He backed out of the driveway and drove off.

I walked to the barn and looked at the packages. They were different shapes and sizes. The bigger packages had cage building materials. I looked for the manual and started reading, to figure out how to build the cheetah cage. The manual pointed out that there was a remote that would help build the cage. I started looking for it among the boxes. I found and opened the smallest box. On the outside was a picture of what the remote looked like and on the inside was a Styrofoam piece holding the remote in place. The remote looked like one of those video game devices young children play with. It had a big screen in the middle, with directional buttons to the left of the screen and two round buttons to the right. It must have been an experimental thing the government wanted to test out.

Next, I tried to figure out the best place to set up the cage. There was an area of land that I owned across the road that was not being used for anything. I guessed that was the piece of land the government wanted me to use for the cheetah. The area was big and spacious and looked about the size of six football fields, in length and width. It looked like a great place where the cheetah would be able to run around and do cheetah things.

The manual told me to put the cage post anchor in a corner of whatever area I decided. Next, I had to hook up the chains and poles to the main cage post so they fed through the post with enough length, according to the dimensions entered into the remote. Once I put in my dimensions and hit enter, the cage post anchored itself to the ground and a line of cage poles and chains shot out of one side and made its way around the border of the vacant land. As the other end made its way back to the main cage post, I noticed three slots opened to receive the chains and poles so that it easily connected. The whole process took about twelve minutes.

After I checked the cage to see if it would hold, I went back to the house, carrying the manuals, boxes, and plastic, and threw the garbage out. Then I went back out to the porch, where the other packages were. I wanted to open them, but couldn't because there was a note on each one saying: *"Please wait to open items until installer comes!!!"*

I really didn't know much about that stuff anyway. It was getting late and I had to get the cows back into their stalls for the night.

This was always very interesting to watch. For some reason, cows know when it's time to come back to the barn for the night. I don't know how they know, but every time I open the back door of the barn, they are all there standing around. I wondered if they thought I was a fool for not knowing what time it was, or if I forgot to come get them again. I chuckled to myself after I opened the door. They came in one-at-a-time and I pointed them into the appropriate stalls. When they were all in, I attached them to their poles so they didn't get away or have anything dangerous happen to them. They had plenty of room to move their heads or lie down when they got tired.

After that, I went back to the house and got ready for bed. I had to get as much sleep as I could to be ready in the morning and do it all over again. For a farmer, life never seems to slow down at all. It's a nonstop job that someone has to do. Once I was in bed, I started to think of all the events of the past couple weeks. I recalled each event as it went through my head. There was a letter from the President. I remembered having that dream during my nap. I wondered if there was a deeper meaning to it. The last thing I remembered was the truck driver with the packages. I had fun building the cage with the remote. That was really cool. As I thought about those events, my mind quickly shifted gears. I focused more about the cheetah being on the land. It was a thought that I normally wouldn't indulge late at night, but it came. I thought about the cheetah being in his cage. The cheetah would be running, playing around, and hanging out in his new habitat. It put a smile on my face and made me feel calm and relaxed about the cheetah situation. I became so calm and relaxed that I drifted softly to sleep.

Day Sixteen

The next morning, I milked the cows before letting them out into the field. I finished the rest of my chores and then headed back to the house. The computer technician came in the afternoon to install the electronic stuff. He was how I pictured a computer technician to be. He was average size and had glasses and dark brown hair. He was in his forties. When he came in, I showed him the set of packages and his jaw dropped. I was afraid if his mouth wasn't attached to his face, it would have gone all the way down to the floor and roll a couple of yards.

We went into the little den room off the kitchen. He quickly started and I watched him connect a bunch of monitors to a little black box. They were being attached to a receiver for the cameras that hung around the caged area for the cheetah. He turned one of the cameras on and pointed a computer monitor in my direction. I was surprised when I saw my face in the monitor.

We both headed outside to the cheetah cage. I thought about what it might be like to be around a cheetah. The only time I was ever near one was at the zoo. The only thing that separated you from the animal was a 4-inch piece of glass. Having a wild animal as a pet was something you imagined as a kid, not as an adult. The computer technician said that we were going to place the cameras in the cage where the cheetah wouldn't notice them. Each camera could see to one hundred feet away. With their zoom feature, they could see an additional one hundred feet. That was pretty neat.

I could keep an eye on the cheetah and see what it was doing. The cameras didn't look like cameras; they looked more like little disco lights.

We headed back to the house, where he showed me how to view the feeds. One monitor could show some camera feeds and the other monitor could pick up the rest. There was a third monitor, for the main computer, which showed every feed. It was neat to see things like this. New technology really impressed me. We've come a long way since the invention of the first camera to Polaroids and now digital. Most of the day was spent installing all the cameras and learning how to use the electronic items to make sure everything worked.

"Thanks for all your hard work. If it had been me installing everything, I may have been here for a long time."

"Not a problem. I was glad to have helped you set up your camera system." He threw his tools back into his truck and drove away.

Day Seventeen

The following afternoon, I heard a knock on the front door. It was another delivery driver, with a freezer. The driver was African American, short, and talked in a southern accent. He had glasses on and a baseball cap with the delivery company's logo. He also had a grey and white goatee.

"I have one big box for a Mr. Ellington."

"Yes sir, that's me," I replied.

"Where would you like your box to go?" I directed him to the milk room. It was a room in the barn where the milk was stored and processed. He put the box by a wall where I could open it later. The man had me sign a piece of paper on his clipboard.

"There you go. Have a good day!"

"Alright now, you take care of yourself." He went back to his truck and went on his way.

The day went by fast and I had to go finish my chores. As I fed the animals, I fixed on watching the calves. It was fun to see them stare at you as if you had something they needed. Some played around their little house. I stopped to play with Duke and Taz for a while. That was always enjoyable. Every other day, I brought the dogs into the house. It was a kind of treat for both of them to come inside.

I think it is cruel to leave an animal outside all the time and never interact with it. I truly think that animals need to be loved and cared for like humans. Not to be treated as objects or items that can be punished or neglected. It really upsets me when I hear stories about animal abuse.

When we got in the house, we all went to bed. It seemed like the day took a toll on all of us, but sometimes there are days like that. Our day is consumed with so many chores that the day becomes endless.

Over the next couple weeks, a man came over to deliver the food for the cheetah. I had him put it all in the freezer.

A man from a gun store also came over.

"Hello, are you Mr. Ellington," the gun man asked.

"Yes sir. What can I do for you?"

He was tall and big. He looked like a redneck but he didn't talk like a redneck. He reminded me of Larry the cable guy. I guess he could have been related.

"My name is Big John, and I am here to show you guns and how to use them so that they can protect you from anything."

We walked out to his truck. It was like a UPS delivery truck except it was all black. We went to the back of the truck and Big John revealed all his equipment to me. He showed me a hunting rifle. The rifle had a scope on the top and it could be used during the day or night. There were some bullets for the rifle that were about two to two and a half inches long.

We moved on to the handheld guns. Most of them were automatic guns. Big John had me hold some of the guns to get a feel of how heavy they are. I was a little blown away when he gave me a Walther PPK. It looked like a little hand gun that anyone could hold, but it had some weight to it.

We continued on to some of the other weapons Big John had

in his truck. I listened and caught on to his tips and advice he was giving pretty quickly. I have never had a gun or fired one before. Big John said that there was a firing range nearby where I could practice if I wanted. He was a member of the range's gun club and members could bring friends to shoot with. There was no charge for the guns, ammo, or use of the firing range. The President had taken care of buying my membership.

When we finished, Big John brought out three large trunks. In one trunk was a set of sedative guns with sedation darts. You could use a special rifle and hand pistol to fire the sedatives. The darts looked like a little injection grey tube with a red feathery brush at the end. In another trunk were a bunch of handheld guns, ranging from pistols to revolvers.

The President and his Cabinet had obviously spent a lot of time arranging all the people and resources to help me out with this. It seemed there was a major concern for my protection. Having firearms on my property made me a little uneasy, but the cheetah is one of the most dangerous animals on the planet. I was very grateful that the government would help me out through this whole process. After all, it was their experiment.

In the last trunk were two more rifles that looked like the one before, and also a bunch of ammo for the rifles. When all was said and done, Big John offered to help me move the trunks into the basement. Once we finished putting the trunks away, he left. I spent the rest of the day, and most of the next, organizing all the guns and rifles.

Day Thirty-One

The final thing that concluded a long month of getting ready was the most amazing thing I've ever experienced. Around noon on March 30, I received a phone call from the Marines. At first, I was wondering *why would the Marines be calling me?* But after talking to them, I realized the answer to my question.

"Hello. This is First Sergeant Second Class Simmons of the Marines. Is Mr. Ellington there?" the voice on the phone asked.

"This is Mr. Ellington. Good afternoon to you, Sergeant."

"Good afternoon to you. I wanted to let you know, that on behalf of the President, we are dispatching a unit of Marines to your land to help you prepare for the arrival of the Wild One."

The Wild One. That must be the codename for the cheetah.

"Well, I appreciate you letting me know, but is it really necessary? My farm is very peaceful and I'm concerned all the noise your unit will bring may cause my animals to act up. They've never had a lot of people around or dealt with all the noises that are going to be made with your unit. Is there any other way of doing this?"

"I'm sorry to inform you that it was the President's call on this matter and there's nothing I can do about. I would also like to inform you that the unit is twenty minutes out from your post and will be arriving. Over and out."

"Thank you, Sergeant Simmons," I said before the phone was hung up. It was clear to me now that this wasn't going to be easy.

I started to head outside and heard a growing noise. It sounded like a war was going on. Not sure if that was the case but, I went out the front door with my hands covering my ears against the intense noise. I looked up and saw four helicopters hovering over my property. Two more went flying by as if chasing something or checking other parts of the land. The animals seemed scared and confused. The dogs barked loudly at the helicopters. As this went on, I saw a Humvee drive up the driveway, with three people in it. The man in the passenger seat got out and waved his arm around in the air like a baseball umpire signaling a homerun. Once his arm finished the signal, the four helicopters rose higher into the sky. That made the noise on the ground a lot less deafening and calmed the animals down as well. The soldier walked up to me.

"Are you Mr. Ellington?" he asked.

"Yeah."

"My name is General Baker and I will be in charge of this part of the operation."

"Okay. Just let me know what you need me to do."

General Baker explained that the Wild One, as they called the cheetah, was about twenty minutes away and he wanted to give me a run-down on how things would go.

"I have a hundred soldiers coming to help with this mission. Our unit has been practicing for one month now and we're ready for any problems that may happen," he said.

"Wow, I didn't know you needed time to get ready for this."

"It was tough in the beginning, but we have it down now. Would you like to watch us do it?"

"Sure. It will be an honor."

We watched for the arrival of the caravan of Marines. They

had five vehicles, not including the Humvee that the General came in. The first vehicle was a jeep truck, with three more soldiers in it, followed by an army truck that had about forty five soldiers. The next vehicle was a semi-truck with what looked like a large animal trailer on it. The trailer was metal and as big as a house. As the semi-truck followed the dirt path, I saw the dark figure of the cheetah. The cheetah paced back and forth as if he expected something to happen. I wasn't sure if wild animals normally did that when they were nervous. For some reason, the cheetah stopped and looked right at me. I could see the orange outline of his eyes within the dark figure in the cage. The cheetah made a sound like a low deep growl.

While we both stared at each other, I had a quick flash of a cheetah with its mouth open, about to bite something. It only lasted a couple of seconds, but once the vision left I felt weak and dropped to my knees. A couple of the soldiers saw me fall and came over to check on me and helped me up. I explained to them that I was okay, but I wasn't sure if they'd understand what happened. Once I got to my feet, I brushed the dust off my pants and watched the truck back up to the opening in the cheetah's caged area.

When the semi-truck stopped, several soldiers carrying weapons ran up and divided into two groups, one on each side of the truck. The General ordered the soldiers to aim their rifles at the trailer door. When they were in position, another soldier climbed on top of the cage. When he got to the top he walked toward the back. As he walked, I smirked a little because this reminded me of the opening scene to that movie with all the dinosaurs in that amusement park.

When the soldier reached the back of the truck, he squatted and waited for the General's next order. The order was given and the soldier started to lift the door on the back of the cage. He raised it higher and higher until you saw the inside of the trailer. The cheetah was all the way in the front of the cage away from the door. I felt my heart pump faster. There was a long pause, and then suddenly I saw the body of the cheetah move toward us from the back of the trailer. When it came to the opening, the cheetah extended his head out to see what was going on. He turned his head to one side and then to the other, analyzing everything outside the trailer. His head came back to looking straight at the field in the enclosed area. The cheetah seemed satisfied with what he saw and jumped down from the cage. Once he got about ten yards away from the opening, we closed the cage. He was secured.

As the cheetah ventured off into his new home, many thoughts rolled through my head. One was that this experiment could work out despite it being potentially dangerous for the animals and me. Another, would this be the last I saw of the General and his army? Many more thoughts jumped around.

When the Marines left, it came time for me to feed the cheetah. My heart raced as fast as a speed boat and I got so nervous that I started to sweat bullets down my face that never seemed to stop. I went to the freezer and grabbed two packages of meat. I grabbed a gun just in case I got into some trouble feeding the cheetah. Next, I walked to the cage and opened the front door. It felt like I was entering a cloudy area and something would come out of nowhere and attack me. Twenty yards away from the door was a trough for the cheetah to eat his meal. I left the door open a little in case I needed a quick escape. Sweat was pouring down my face and I could feel that sick feeling you get when you are about to regurgitate. My job was to get to the trough and back in one piece with no problems.

I walked to the trough and noticed the cheetah was ten yards away from me on a hill near a tree. He was watching me deliver his meal. I stopped and pointed the gun at him. Caught in a scary situation, my hand was shaking the gun around. I have never fired a gun in my life and was starting to panic at this point, so I waited a while to see what the cheetah would do. All the cheetah did was sit there. Not sure if anything would happen, I continued on to the trough with the two packs of meat in one hand and the gun in the other still fixed on the cheetah. Twenty yards seemed to take a long time to walk. When I finished, I went back to the door. Before I closed the door, I looked back to see where the cheetah was. He was still in the same spot. I didn't wait for the cheetah to decide if it wanted to eat or not. I had other things to do.

Day Forty

A week or two after the cheetah arrived; a reporter came to my house. I never really liked news or reporters at all. I felt they always took advantage of what a person said and turned it into something else. I hate when people manipulate others. It really makes me mad.

Anyhow, I wasn't surprised that a reporter came. In the back of my mind, I knew it would happen sooner or later. To be honest, I wished that nobody knew about it. That would have made my life easier; no publicity, lies, scandals or things associated with falsified terminology. Don't get me wrong. I don't mind having been informed of the news. I just wished that the news would be more truthful.

The reporter knocked on the front door and I went over to it. Bright sunlight poured into the dark shadows near the door as I opened it. I had to cover my eyes and squint to see who was there. Once my eyes adjusted, the dark figure transformed into a woman on my porch.

"Mr. Ellington?" the young lady asked.

"Who the heck are you?" I usually respond that way when someone knocks on my door. I'm not sure why I do that, but it comes naturally. I probably heard that a lot from a relative when I was younger.

"My name is Kansas City Jones, or K. C., and I work for the Arizona Chronicle."

"Oh, come on man," I said.

She continued, "We believe there is a wild animal living on the farm. Do you mind if I ask you a few questions?"

I was a little perplexed that she didn't know all the information. I assumed that a reporter would've had more information about the cheetah by now.

"You mean you don't know what animal it is?" I asked.

"Well, we know it's a wild animal, but we don't know what kind."

I stood there for a moment with my arms crossed, and scratched my chin with one of my hands. It puzzled me that no one figured it out yet. I looked into her brown eyes and my tough shell broke.

"Okay," I said. "I have to admit I don't really care that much about the media. I will answer your questions, but you have to promise me something. If I give you what you want to know, you must keep the information between you and me."

"That can't happen. Even if I were able to keep it secret, eventually the information would come out."

"I guess you're right. I just don't want a mass of people over here looking for the cheetah and doing things to it. I am not for making a wild animal any more wild and dangerous than it already is."

"It's a cheetah! Wow, that's great. I mean, wow a cheetah on a farm. May I come in, please?"

"Oh, my! Where are my manners today? Yes, please do. Can I get you anything to drink? I have water, tea, or juice."

"I will have some water, please."

I showed her where the living room was and told her to make herself comfortable. She sat on the couch which faced the two chairs that were in the middle of the living room. I walked into the kitchen and got her water. I handed the drink to her and sat in one of the chairs. While she drank, I got a better look at her. She made me think of those girls in high school, the popular ones that looked like goddesses of the Nile. They were so beautiful, they made almost everyone stop and look at them as they walked by.

K.C. looked to be in her late thirties and had dark brown curly hair. She had a red dress on with a black belt around her waist, not that I was looking. It was right there in front, you couldn't miss it. Her eyes were like two light blue marbles with chocolate chips in the middle. She had skin that reminded me of cappuccino. It was hard to see if she wore makeup or not. She was pretty, regardless of makeup.

"Well, uh, what can I do for you?" I started off saying. Her beauty made me a bit nervous. She reached for her purse, which matched her dress, and started digging for something. I always wondered why women had to have the same color purse, shoes, dress, makeup, bags and other accessories. Guys don't need a lot of things with the same color. As I pondered that, my eyes returned to K. C. still digging in her purse. Her digging around caught my attention even more. *What was she looking for?*

"A-ha!" she said. She put the purse down with one hand, and held a little tape recorder in the other. She set the tape recorder on the coffee table and pushed a button to start recording. Once I saw the little dials start moving, my stomach got that weird, butterfly feeling. I was afraid I'd mess up my words.

Her first question was, "Who are you and what is it you do?"

The first question kickoff, I thought to myself. I responded with, "My name is James Ellington and I'm a dairy farmer."

"Is it true that you have other animals living here?"

Chuckling to myself I said, "Yes. Besides dairy cows, I have bunnies and two dogs."

"Is it true you also have a new animal on your farm?" she added.

"I guess I do now. I hoped not to draw attention to the fact that a wild animal is living on the property across from the farm. Over there, it cannot harm the other animals, and everyone is safe."

"Why would any human, let alone a farmer, want to live with a wild animal?"

I chuckled again. In the back of my mind I thought, *yes, why would anyone want to live with a wild animal?*

"Well, I was given the opportunity to be a part of something so special; I still cannot believe that it happened. I think I'm the first person to be used in this situation. It's a great honor."

"What is mysterious about this situation and what makes it feel like such an honor?" K.C. asked.

Oh. You are really good at this, aren't you, I thought to myself. She seemed to know what she wanted and how to get it. "At this juncture, I'm not allowed to let you know. I made a commitment and want to stay loyal to the government for their trust in me."

She nodded her head as if to say she understood. "As a farmer, does taking care of a wild animal add more work to what you already do?"

"It certainly does require more work. I'm not sure how much more work it is, but it is like having a child in the family or being in a relationship. Once you add another person, animal or thing to your life, you'll have to start to do more work than before."

"Have you had any concerns about living with the wild animal? Like the possibility of escape and damage to other farms?"

"Well, I guess I have a little bit of concerns, now. I'm trying not to worry about these things, but when you start to worry, you take the fun out of everything else. Let's say someone loves statistics a lot and because he loves them so much he starts thinking about the odds of things that can happen to him in his life. He is basically living on chance and worried that one of his statistics will eventually happen or he will find another incident where the odds are greater or lesser than the original incident and he might try to avoid those incidents and protect himself. I think you have to live life the way you want to and take a risk once in a while. You are not truly living if you are analyzing everything around you. I try not to let those things bother me. Yes, there is a chance the wild animal will do those things you mentioned. And there is a chance he may not. I guess we will cross that bridge when we get there."

"What information do you have about taking care of wild animals? Who has provided any help or information to you?"

"I've read some books and I also have a farm, so I have a lot of experience working with animals. I know what to do. It may be a challenge taking care of a new animal, but life is full of challenges that we all must face and we may succeed or fail, depending on the actions we take. I would say that if you aren't taking any risks in your life, you aren't really living."

"Wow, pretty bold there, but I can see that assessment. By the way, what is the animal?"

"It is a cheetah."

"Well, thanks for your time Mr. Ellington and thank you for your responses. I hope to keep in touch with you. I do have one more question and then I must be on my way. Have you given any thought to adding more cheetahs to your farm? After all, the cheetah may get lonely."

What did that mean? I thought for a while. K.C. really threw me a curve ball. I was at a loss for words. Why would she say something like that? Did she know something or was that one of those things you say and forget you said it. I never really thought about it. Having another cheetah on the farm? Something didn't feel right as I tried to squander up an answer to her question. A different thought popped in my head. It could be she wasn't thinking about the cheetah, maybe she was thinking about me. That seems weird, some forty-year-old worried about some seventy-year-old. Still the fact that did matter was that I've been alone most of my life. Occasionally someone would come over and visit me; not very often. Could it be she also referred to me? She took another sip of her water.

"To answer your question, I'm not sure what will happen in the future. It's funny to me that I've heard everything happens for a reason. I believe that, though I'm not sure why or how I will ever know. It could all depend on how it goes with the cheetah. I don't know for sure." That was my response to her final question. K.C. pushed the stop button on her recorder. She finished her water and grabbed the recording device to put in her purse. Next, she rose from her chair and I got up from mine to show respect.

"Thanks again for your time," she said.

"No problem, I am happy to have answered your questions." We exited the living room and headed to the front door. I opened the door for her and followed her to her car.

When she was gone, I got back to my chores around the farm and had time to feed the cheetah. The memory of K. C. was still dancing in my head so much that I forgot to check the calf houses for cleaning and feeding until it was dinner time.

The day slipped away and night crept in. I made sure to finish putting the cows in the barn before going to the house. I made myself dinner and decided to watch some television. I waited to see what the weather was going to be like, and if anything interesting had happened around the area. As I waited for the weather, the news was on and one story caught my attention.

"This just in: local resident, James Ellington, of the Winchester area, has volunteered to help the government with an experiment. The experiment is designed to see if humans and wild animals can live together in the same area. The site of this experiment is Mr. Ellington's farm, home to cows, rabbits and a couple of dogs. The animal that will be joining them as part of the experiment is, in fact, a wild cheetah. Much more information is still to be determined, but thanks to several classified sources we have confirmed that the animal is on the farm right now and it..."

I turned off the television. I knew it was going to happen. Now I had no control over the situation. I was upset that the news anchor gave information about the animal and its location. I didn't want people to know a cheetah was close by. Some people might cause a stampede rushing to the farm to see it. I didn't need a mass of people coming to my farm and exciting the other animals. The cheetah was still a wild and dangerous animal. A lot of people at the farm might cause the cheetah to do weird and crazy stuff, which could cause an accident of some kind. I really wished that information wasn't out there. Worrying about it now wouldn't help. Whatever happened was going to happen. There was no way to stop it.

Day Forty-One

The next morning I did not want to wake up. I really hated that feeling. We rarely allow ourselves the full satisfaction of staying in bed. Instead, we ignore our bodies and fight through the haze. It's a long struggle we all go through each and every morning. I forced myself from my horizontal state and pulled my blanket off. I usually sit in a position where my legs can dangle over the side of the bed and hang there for a minute or two as I try to wake up.

Eventually I made it to the kitchen. I tried to figure out what to make myself for breakfast. I looked in the refrigerator and the cabinets and came up with eggs, toast and coffee. As my food cooked and my coffee percolated, I went out to the porch and grabbed my paper. I must let you in on a little secret. If you ever get the chance to wake up really early and see what the world looks like between five a.m. and seven a.m., you should try it. Arizona at this hour is a wonderful sight. It's a moment you'd want to last lifetime.

The sky was an array of colors that looked like an artist had thrown them up into the air and let them stick. The sun's rays peeked through the trees and touched the cold ground from the night before. The dew rose up and filled the air, sweetly fragrant.

I breathed deep and embraced the world around me. It was a wonderful view created by God, whose knowledge is beyond our fathoming.

When I was done looking at the incredible display that existed outside my house, I headed back inside for breakfast and the paper

I finished washing my dishes and made sure I put them away. My parents taught us at a young age to wash up after yourself that it became like a reflex and I also like to be organized. I went back to the table and grabbed the paper to take out to the porch to finish. When I sat down on my porch chair, my eyes opened wide as I read the following headline:

SPOTTED ANIMAL AMONG SPOTTED COWS
By Skip Valley

Cowlic- In an area known for its farming, a new face is among the cow pastures. A large cheetah has been seen roaming the fields of a local farm this week. The vacant piece of land, now the home of the cheetah, belongs to dairy farmer and Cowlic native, James Ellington.

It's unknown what the cheetah is doing in the vacant area. Within the past few weeks there has been a lot of traffic going to and from the farm. Many within Pima County have been making speculations about having a wild animal in the area. Some neighbors are okay with it, but others have a different opinion.

"A wild animal in this area could be dangerous," says Kathy Burnheart, Mayor of Sells. "I'm not sure what Mr. Ellington was thinking when he decided to have a cheetah live on his farm. I'm worried about the safety of the people in our community. I really think he should have asked around before making a big decision like this." Several unnamed sources have witnessed deliveries made to Ellington's farm and one

has seen a large Marine caravan that may have had a hand in helping with delivering the cheetah. Still, it's hard to say who is behind this. It could be local zoos, the National Wildlife Organization or other government agencies.

"This is an unusual situation. I'm both happy and a little bit scared." James said in an interview when asked how he felt about the whole ordeal. Mr. Ellington has cows, rabbits and two dogs on his property and is taking every precaution necessary with the cheetah.

I knew K.C. couldn't keep the information to herself. What was I supposed to do now? I knew a lot of people would come to see the cheetah, so while I tried to figure out what to do to handle the situation, I headed out to the barn.

The phone in the barn rang

"Hello."

"Hey James," the woman's voice sounded familiar. "It's K.C."

Not certain what to do, I panicked. I felt like a little boy receiving a phone call from a girl for the first time. You get that weird feeling in the pit of your stomach. It's like a bunch of butterflies flying around. I was a little bit upset that word about of the cheetah got out and I didn't want to let my anger get the best of me when talking to K.C. Trying to be nice and cool, I responded with, "Oh, hi."

"Look…James…I'm sorry I let your information out, but someone in the office took my recorder and shared it with other news stations. I really didn't mean to have this happen. I'm sorry I let you down." K.C. started to cry. I wasn't sure why. It could be that she was very upset she broke a promise. Most people don't realize they've broken a promise until they're confronted with what they've done.

"Hey, it's okay. I knew the story was going to get out. I shouldn't have made you promise something you couldn't have kept. I'm sorry, too. You're forgiven."

"Thanks," K.C. replied, still crying. "Is there anything I can do for you now that the whole country knows?"

"I don't think I need anything right now, but thanks for the offer."

"Okay, if you think of something or need anything just give me a call, okay?"

"Will do."

"Alright. I got to go now. You take care of yourself."

"Okay, you as well. Bye."

"Goodbye James."

She hung up. I stood there for a while with the phone still close to my ear before returning it back to the phone stand.

What I am I supposed to do now? I was sure half the country was on their way to the farm. I wasn't sure what was going to happen. All I could think was I needed help. I knew K.C. wanted to help but she was one person. I was going to need more than one person to help me with this dilemma.

I walked out of the barn and tried to devise a plan for the visitors who would come by to see the cheetah. At one point, I stopped and looked at the road. The road that connected to my driveway was long. Part of it you couldn't see because of a big hill. You could only see a vehicle coming once it reached the top of the hill. As you passed the driveway, the road continued for thirty yards and then there was a stop sign. You could only turn left or right. I looked at the hill to see if anything was coming.

I noticed that I did that a lot when I headed toward the house. I wonder if other people ever did that: walk toward their house and look up the road to see if anything is coming. It is like we are all waiting for something to happen. When it comes, we have this sigh of relief. If nothing comes, we move on, but we keep looking till something happens.

I looked at the hill and there was nothing. When I got to the porch, I heard a vehicle in the distance. My ears amazed some people. They called me "Dog Ears" because I could hear things from far away. I looked back to make sure I was right and to see what kind of car it was. I'm not sure why men are fascinated to see cars go by, but it's in our blood and it really gets us excited.

The vehicle was a military hum-v, carrying two Marines. As the hum-v came closer, I thought I recognized the Marine who was riding. I wasn't quite sure because it was hard to see from that far away. The hum-v made its way up the driveway and stopped right in front of my porch, where I was standing. When the dust cleared, I was surprised to see who was sitting in the passenger seat.

"Long time no see, eh General?" I said to the general who helped put the cheetah on the farm. I was happy to see him, but a little bit confused as to why he was here.

"Well, well, well Mr. Ellington," the General responded in a joking kind of manner. "Same to you, I suppose. It's good to know that you're still in one piece. I got a little concerned about you."

"Well, you don't have to worry about me. I can take care of myself and have been for quite some time. By the way, what brings you to my neck of the woods?"

"Well Mr. Ellington, the President got a hold of the big news that somebody found out about this top-secret operation and was certain a big mass of people would be on their way. The President had us come by to make sure nothing happened and no one got into trouble. We developed a plan that we think might be able to help out in this situation."

"That's great! I wasn't sure what to do about the people coming. I've never dealt with a situation like this before. I'm eager to hear what kind of plan you've come up with."

"Well, I will say there are going to be a lot of people coming this way to see the cheetah. Think of it like this, you own a burger shop and are going to give out free burgers. A lot of people are going to come. We need to make sure we keep people and the cheetah safe in a controlled area."

"Sounds like you and your men have a pretty good plan how to handle the situation. If there's anything I can do to help, please let me know."

"Alright, will do, Mr. Ellington," the General said.

I wasn't quite sure that the Marines had dealt with a situation like this before, but there wasn't anyone else I could really count on or turn to. The people were coming and time was getting short.

The next two hours seemed busy for the Marines. More and more came to the farm. There were more than when the cheetah arrived. The Marines hopped out of their vehicles, and made their way to the General, who gave out their assignments. Some kept busy putting up tents for the others to work or rest in. The General and other high ranking soldiers were trying to set up a perimeter around the cheetah area. What went on made me laugh because I'd never been around much military-type stuff. Seeing one marine come and go, and then another doing the exact same thing a couple seconds later, just seemed too funny.

After another hour, it looked like the Marines settled down a bit, as if they were ready for whatever was coming. They blocked off the entrance to the farm and to the cheetah area. It seemed like there were a thousand Marine soldiers standing around me and the whole farm. Everywhere you looked there they were. It didn't take long for people to arrive. It was like a parade. A big posse of cars came over the top of the hill and started down it. It looked like the line of cars never ended. The vehicles ranged from cars, trucks, and vans to SUVs. The traffic kept coming. I started to feel nervous, like my insides were pumping out bullets of sweat. I wondered where all these cars were supposed to park. My driveway was blocked off by the Marines.

Within a matter of minutes, the vehicles were all parked up and down the main road. It was like a big festival came to my barn. I saw families of all different sizes; old and young; couples, parents, children, and even some reporters made their way over to the cheetah. The mass of people seemed like a lot for the Marines to handle. But the people knew they were being watched and made sure they didn't do anything wrong. Still, more and more people came. They had to park a good mile away and walk, but that wasn't an issue for them. They wanted to see the cheetah, and be able to say, "I was this close to the cheetah" or "I got to see the cheetah do this or that."

As the crowd got bigger and eventually grew around the enclosed area, it was harder for people to see the cheetah. It didn't help that the Marines were standing in front of the enclosed area, protecting the cheetah and the people from harm. I noticed that some of the people brought binoculars, cameras and other viewing devices to catch a glimpse of the cheetah. Some children were on their parent's shoulders to get a better look. The General was right, the place was packed. I never thought I would see a lot of people in one place just to see a cheetah.

I was very grateful that the Marines helped out with the crowd. It was a crazy and hectic situation that seemed to be under control now. I decided to get on with my farm work. As I mentioned, there were reporters around, trying to get more information from me. They brought their camera crews and also had photographers taking pictures of me. I felt awkward while I worked but I tried not to let that bother me.

By supper time, the crowd was still all around the cheetah. It seemed to me that the crowd got bigger than before. Now I had to go feed the cheetah. I made sure that the other animals were fed first. I went to the freezer in the barn to get his food. I grabbed a pouch, which was a two-quart plastic bag of food. When I started to make my way toward the cheetah, I was accompanied by two lines of five Marines on each side of me. I guess the General wanted to make sure I was safe as well. We walked into the crowd and the reporters surrounded us like a bunch of birds trying to get at something. I didn't say anything as the reporters kept asking questions. The Marines told people to stand aside so we could get through. We stopped at the entrance of the cage, which was the only place you could get to the cheetah trough quickly.

I noticed that the crowd was watching the cheetah, crouched on one of the hills. They must have known something was about to happen. I stared at the pouch of food in my hands for a while. When I blinked, the pouch changed into what appeared to be the decapitated head of a calf. I wiped my eyes for a second or two. It got silent, as if I was entering another vision and everyone around me was talking, but I never heard anything. I looked back at the pouch of food, only it wasn't food anymore. I was completely shocked and stunned at the sight still in my hand. I couldn't believe it. I thought I was dreaming. *Could this have been another vision? Was the vision telling me I was feeding the cheetah the head of a calf?*

I was now sweating profusely, as if I just awoke from a nightmare. But the problem was that I was awake. I rubbed my eyes again, trying to block out the image of the calf's head. I blinked for a minute or two and looked back down and saw the pouch.

I let out a sigh of relief. The noise of the crowd returned as well. I was a little unstable from the vision, so I leaned on the cage and tried to catch my breath. Was I going crazy?

"Mr. Ellington! Are you okay?" one of the Marines asked.

"I'm alright, just a little light-headed from being around the crowd." I couldn't tell him what really happened. I wasn't sure he'd believe me. I got my strength back and opened the door to the cheetah area.

Now, I was scared. I had that sensation you get when you're walking alone at night and you feel you're being followed, but nobody's there. Your heart starts pumping faster and you feel each beat in your neck. Well, that was exactly how I felt seeing the cheetah look straight at me. The trough was halfway between us. The crowd started to make some noises as I began to walk towards it. I could hear little squeaks or panicked expressions as I got closer. I carried an automatic handgun in a holster. I was not taking any chances with this animal. I wasn't about to die. I moved closer and saw the cheetah lick the sides of his mouth. I assumed he knew I was carrying his dinner.

I got to the trough, opened the pouch of food and dumped it in. I put my hand on the gun, preparing to pull it out if needed, and backed away, never letting the cheetah out of my sight. While all this went on, I heard *ohhhs* and *ahhhs* from the crowd. I opened the cage door and walked back into the crowd and away with the Marines around me.

Over the next few weeks, people came from all over the country to see the cheetah. I knew this from looking at all the license plates. The size of the crowds started to get smaller. It was hard for newcomers to park their cars close because of all the people around the cheetah area. I remember once, when the weather got colder, that the people huddled around one another to stay warm. I chuckled to myself. They reminded me of a bunch of penguins I saw on television. The penguins huddled together as a group where the male penguins were taking care of the eggs, keeping them warm. They could withstand temperatures of about negative eighty degrees. That was without the wind, mind you. I was amazed that God created an animal to withstand those types of temperatures.

K.C. came over every chance she could to help out. She was definitely a big help during those first few weeks. She helped by talking to the reporters and gave them whatever information they needed. I was glad to have somebody deal with them. Otherwise, they would keep bothering me. When she wasn't helping, she would be back in downtown Cowlic living in her one-room apartment and working for the Chronicle.

As time went on and weeks changed into months, the weather

changed dramatically. The clouds rolled in a lot and you barely saw the sun anymore. People still came to see the cheetah. When the summertime came around, I felt more sympathetic towards the Marines. The Marines had been around for about eleven months now and had a tough schedule. The warm summer heat must have taken a toll on them. I know if I was standing around like them for many hours, I would be sweating up a storm so to speak. I tried to figure how long some of the Marines had been helping out with crowd control. Everyday some of the Marines did a shift-change at 3:00 p.m. in the day to get rest. I was glad I was not a Marine. Don't get me wrong, I know it is a great honor to serve our country, but I just never thought I could do it. I appreciated those who served America to keep it protected.

It was the following fall when the crowd showed a major decrease in attendance. I couldn't believe that it finally happened. I wasn't sure if I would be able to get on with my life again. I say that, because I was never a very talkative person and when I am around a big group of people, I get nervous and don't know what to say. I wasn't sure if the crowd wanted me to give a speech or something or if the Marines answered their questions. Either way at least the crowd left.

Day Four Hundred Twenty

The Cheetah had been living with me for about fourteen months. It took me a while to get used to working it into my daily duties, but I was able to fit in the time I needed to take care of him. Feeding him became such a familiar routine that it felt like clockwork. One thing bugged me though; what to do next?

During the fourteen months I'd spent with the cheetah, a lot happened. People still came to see him, but not as much as before. I was glad the crowd size had gone down. It made me less nervous knowing that only half as many eyes were watching as before. It was certainly awkward for me to feed the cheetah with what seemed like a million sets of eyes watching my every move. To be focused on him was a little difficult as well, but I was relieved.

Around feeding time during the last part of the fourteen months, I tried something else. I tried to be friendly with the cheetah. I thought that might make him feel more welcome and help him adjust to his new habitat. I went through the door and I made my way to the trough. It was funny, though. It felt like nothing could happen until right before I did it. Thus, I got the butterflies again. With the meat in-hand and the cheetah in front of me, my heart raced before I made my move.

"Hey there little fella. I am going to feed you now, okay?" *Boy, this feels idiotic.* I was glad not many people saw this. Why was I talking to an animal that would never talk back? I really felt embarrassed that I was talking like a little child.

"Sorry, maybe I should talk to you in a normal voice here," I said. All the cheetah did was look at me. I tried again. "I hope we can get along together. It would be great if we could hang out." Still, he didn't move from his position. I didn't think talking was going to help, so I made a move closer to him with my hand out. The cheetah noticed my movement and he moved his head down low to the ground, making a rattling noise, and showing his teeth letting me know he didn't want anything to do with me. I stopped pursuing him. I didn't want to make him uncomfortable. I put the food in the trough and made my way back to the farm. There had to be a way to make the cheetah feel more friendly and welcome to this place. What could it be?

Another thing that happened was the Marines presence shrunk. Boy, it felt like yesterday that the Marines were setting up for the big mass of people coming. Tents here, troops standing there. It seemed as if my farm turned into a military base. I once joined a group of Marines during one of their marching exercises. I came outside from the house and because I was already used to their ways and formations that I, just like a reflex, started following them around and participated in the daily activities. I asked to become a Marine, but thank God the General refused my request to join and brought me back to my senses. I didn't think the animals would have been okay with First Sergeant Second Class, James Ellington. I could picture the dogs with their heads tilted to one side as if they were pointing out that I was crazy, or even the calves with that "who cares" look. What happened next was what really caught me by surprise.

When the Marines started to down-size, I noticed lately, that I would be sitting in my den around the monitors with all the cameras around the cheetah's living area. It seemed to happen more frequently. I clicked my mouse at one of the cameras in the caged area that was pointed at the cheetah and view it full screen on the main monitor. Once it was set, I would watch the cheetah and think for hours. What am I doing? What is he thinking about? It would go on and on until I got to the point where I couldn't remember what I was thinking about in the first place. I sat there looking at the cheetah trying to figure out if there was more to this experiment.

One morning, I got an idea. I went back to the letter the President sent me. What I was looking for was a return address that would help me connect with the President. I figured I would send him a letter. There had to be more to this experiment than I knew. I mean, living with the cheetah seemed easy, but what was the experiment supposed to be? I needed answers.

Dear Mr. President,

Thank you for the opportunity to be a part of your experiment. It is a great honor to help. Which brings me to my main concern of the matter: what is the purpose of the experiment? Did you tell me before and I missed it? I am not sure if I am doing what you wanted or not. If you could please enlighten me, it would be very useful to know what you plan to accomplish. Thanks again for the opportunity to be a part of what you hope to accomplish.

Sincerely,

James Ellington

It seemed simple, I guess. I wasn't really sure how to write a proper letter to the President.

After I sent it, I received another letter within a couple of weeks. I was really excited to see what the President had to say. It was like the butterfly feeling in your stomach, only this time it was not as active, or should I say, fluttery. I opened up the letter.

Dear Mr. Ellington,

Thank you for being active and willing to join our experiment to see if wild animals can coexist with humans. The point of the experiment is to coexist with each other. You can play with it, feed it, take care of it, and anything else you are able to do with it. We would like you to send a brief summary each week to show your progress in encounters with the cheetah. Think of this: you and the cheetah are living in an animal sanctuary helping the greater good of the country. You can send your summary to the address on the envelope, along with any other requests.

Sincerely,

Leo Schmidt

President of the United States

Day Five Hundred and Seventy-Seven

Lately, I noticed a lot of weird things happening around me. It was hard to explain, but I felt like Ray Kinsella in *Field of Dreams*. I kept hearing this voice around me on the farm. It seemed out of place at first, but then it started to get creepy.

The voice, a creepy whisper, kept saying, "Get another one!" When I first heard the voice, I looked around to see who was talking to me. Nobody was there. Where was the voice coming from? I wasn't sure what "another one" was. I waited for a minute or two before I went back to what I was doing. Then I heard it again.

"Get another one." Ohhh, the chills and willies were all over me. This had to stop. I wasn't quite sure how to stop the voice, but I was determined to try. I thought I'd talk back to it.

"Get another one." The voice said a third time. I wasn't sure if I felt more awkward talking to the voice than the cheetah.

"Hello?" No response, so I continued. "Hey, is this some kind of joke or something? I hear you, but I'm not sure what you mean. Could you please explain to me what *another one* is?" I finished and waited for a response. Nothing happened. The emptiness surrounded me with nothing but the blowing wind.

"Get another one!"

Trying to outsmart it I said, "Ha, I know where you are!" But I didn't know where it was. "This game is getting quite old for me and I don't have time to figure out the riddle." I was upset. I continued on with the barn work and ignored the voice.

After the voice came, I started to get visions that could be linked to it. One vision I had, was where I was feeding the cheetah. I walked up to the trough and dumped out his food. When I was done, I looked to see where he was. When I saw him, I noticed that there was another cheetah next to him. I quickly took my glasses off to rub my eyes, and put them back on. When my sight refocused, I saw there was only one cheetah. *That was weird.* That continued for a while Every time I fed the cheetah, I would see another cheetah, right there, plain as day. But when I rubbed my eyes, the second cheetah had disappeared.

While that happened, I also had a couple of dreams, too. One dream was where I sat at a table and someone handed me a present. It was a box wrapped in cheetah wrapping paper and had a brown bow on it. I opened it and looked inside. I couldn't see what was inside but I know I was excited about it. Then I received another box, but this one had black wrapping paper. And when I opened it, I looked in and I turned my face from it. I could not bear to see what was on the inside. I was absolutely scared of what was inside that box. I woke up after that dream all wet and sweaty.

Another dream I had was more intense. I was on my way to feed the cheetah. The sky was cloudy, *really cloudy.* The ground was dark brown with yellow strands of grass coming out. I got to the trough and put the food in, while I looked for the cheetah. I found him and then I saw the second cheetah. Then there were more and more cheetahs popping up all around me, as far as the eye could see. I couldn't move. I was stuck within the pride of cheetahs. I looked around and was able to find a way out of the surrounding cheetahs. There was a path that would lead me to the door of the caged area, but if I was going to be able to get to it, I would have to make a run for it now.

As I was running for the door, one of the cheetahs noticed and started running towards me. The others saw that cheetah running, and they all joined in chasing me. I ran as hard as I could as the pride of cheetahs ran after me. As I tried to open the door, a cheetah jumped into the air and pounced on me. That was when I woke up. Wet and sweaty, and my heart raced, I choked on a breath as if I'd just come back to life.

Late at night, I also found myself looking at the monitors showing the cheetah area. I would watch the cheetah for hours and hours. Sometimes, I watched so long that the next thing I knew, the sun was up and the rooster was crowing. I had to have a lot of coffee those days.

I saw K.C. every now and then. She showed up dressed like a TV farm girl. She reminded me of Daisy Duke, with her short blue jeans that came down to her thighs. She also wore maroon-brown cowboy boots and a red flannel shirt like Al Borland's, only smaller. The bottom was rolled up into a knot in front, showing her stomach. Her dark brown hair hung loose which I didn't mind. I would smile every time she came by. I didn't know why I would do that, but it felt like I was stronger or happier when I saw her. She would check on me to see if I was okay and all that other stuff. I decided to share with her what was happening lately.

"Hey, K. C., can I ask you something?"

"Sure, what can I do for you?" She replied in her southern accent.

"There have been a lot of strange things going on lately."

"Like what?"

"I heard a weird voice on the farm a while ago and it sounded like a whisper. The voice would say, *get another one*. It's scaring me because I am alone. I know nobody around here would pull a prank on me, so I'm not sure what it means. I've also found myself feeling sympathetic toward the cheetah, because all he does is sit near that tree and doesn't move much. I wonder if there is something wrong with him."

"Could you try playing with it?"

"I've tried interacting with the cheetah, but he doesn't seem interested. I don't know what else I can do. Do you think he's okay?"

"Well, I'm not a veterinarian." She looked at me with her mouth open, almost like she figured something out. Then, she blinked her eyes and shook her head. "Do you remember what you said the other day?"

"No, what?" I asked.

"You said that everything happens for a reason, right?"

"I do recall that," I said.

"Now, I think that your dreams and visions mean something. I have a weird feeling that you need to get another cheetah."

That was it. That was what I needed to do. K.C. figured it out. I thanked her and told her that in my next report I would add the idea of another cheetah.

The time came for me to send the next report to the White House. The President wanted me to use a notebook with easy to rip out pages and write in it the date, what I did on that day with the cheetah, and the cheetah's reaction to my encounter. With the report I attached this note to it.

Dear Mr. President,

This is Mr. Ellington with my next report. I have made several attempts to get close to the cheetah, but so far he doesn't want anything to do with me. I noticed that he doesn't move around much and seems lonely (from my perspective). I think it may be beneficial if the cheetah could interact with another cheetah. Hopefully, this request doesn't jeopardize the experiment. This might help the cheetah and who knows, it may help all mankind. I await your decision and hope you think this is a good idea. Thanks for your time.

Sincerely,

James Ellington

I had K.C. look over the note to see if it was acceptable. I like to make sure things look nice and neat. She said it looked good. I folded the note along with the report and put it into the mailbox.

"Now, all we have to do is wait for a response," I said.

K.C. looked at me and smiled for a brief moment.

It took a while for a response to come; about two weeks. When I saw the letter, I called K.C. and told her to come over as soon as possible. When she arrived, I opened it up and started to read it. I read it to myself quietly.

"Would you stop reading the letter to yourself and read it for everyone to hear?"

"Oops. I'm sorry about that." I didn't realize K.C. didn't like that, but I guess that is upsetting to someone who is waiting the same response as you are. I started it again, this time out loud.

Dear Mr. Ellington,

Thank you for your report. It was good to hear that you are making progress with the cheetah. We were also glad to hear that the experiment has not failed.

The primary goal for this experiment was to see if one person could handle training one dangerous animal. That is why the Cabinet and I thought another cheetah would cause more chaos and stress. We weren't sure how well the experiment would go or if there might have been some complications, but with what information you have given us and if you think you can handle another cheetah, we've decided to accept your request. Our researchers have begun a search for a female cheetah. We are also making sure the female cannot have babies. Your safety and the safety of your farm is a concern of ours.

The Cabinet and I are concerned that you will be doing a lot by yourself, so we think you should have some help. I've talked with Kansas City Jones, and she seems more than happy to help out. You will also receive a special service, since you will be unable to do many things while taking care of the animals. The service will be provided at no cost. Through it, you'll receive deliveries to your house of things like groceries, home repair items, clothing, and other necessities. I have included the call number at the end of this letter and someone will help you get started.

Thanks again and good luck to you both.

Sincerely,

Leo Schmidt

President of the United States

I put the letter down and stood there thinking to myself. I wasn't sure if the President knew that it wasn't that hard taking care of a cheetah. Maybe having two cheetahs might be harder. K.C. looked like she was about to burst from happiness, the way girls sometimes do. Her lips curled over each other and she made those noises like little snickers or shrieks. I looked at her because her noises distracted me. I was afraid she might explode soon.

"Are you okay?"

She let her excitement out with a big, "Ahhh! Did you hear what the letter said?"

"What?" I replied as if I missed something.

"The President granted your request! He even gave you his phone number in the postscript! Isn't that great?"

"Yes, but there is something I didn't count on. The President wants you to help me."

Day Six Hundred and Twelve

"Are you sure you want to do this?" I asked.

K.C. looked down for a minute in thought. I was upset. I felt like K.C. went right around my back to make sure she could help in the experiment. My anger made me think that K.C. was up to something.

"I want to be able to help you here on the farm. You're all alone and need some help, but you're afraid of asking for that help."

She pleaded her side. It took a while for her side to sink in. *I don't ask for help? She was right.* It took a little courage, but I finally conceded the fact that I needed help and she was the help I needed.

"Well, welcome to the farm." Her face went from an unsure look to really excited and she started making those girly noises. I explained to K.C. that it would be better if she lived on the farm. That way, she didn't have to wake up early and drive here or leave really late with limited time for sleep. The animals would get used to her and we could get more work done. She said she needed some time to pack her things before she moved in.

About three days passed before K.C. came back. Her whole car looked like it was about to explode with all of the items in it. When she packs, she *packs*. She arrived around suppertime. While we were unpacking her car, I wasn't quite sure it would be able to fit in the house. Her car was jam-packed with what I guess is called, "girl necessities." Things like makeup, tampons, lingerie, basically a bunch of girl stuff. We put her things down in the den. I put a bed in it, along with a table for her to sit at and work or read something. There was a bathroom nearby where she could put her essentials in and make it her own. I had time to fix everything up before she came. I wanted it to look nice for her. It was the least I could do. I don't get many visitors and besides, it was like a little farm-warming present so she wouldn't feel homesick.

We took a break to have supper. It seemed like a good night and plus with K.C. moving in I decided to have a special dinner planned for her and made pot-roast with mashed potatoes and bread. Mmmmm. While we ate, we talked about things like who would cook certain meals and I told her this house was hers now, so she should treat it that way. We had a ball talking and laughing. The animals probably thought we were having a party or something. Well, all things must come to an end though; it was time to go to bed. I'm not really picky about things, but I do enjoy getting as many hours of sleep as I can. As we both made ourselves ready for bed, we bid each other a pleasant, "Good Night."

The next day, I got up earlier than K.C. and I decided to give her some beauty sleep, as my sister called it, because soon she would not get much, living on the farm. She would have to get up early like me to help do the chores. I also got up early to have some time to show her around and to talk about things. When she got up, I made breakfast. We had a big-time breakfast celebrating K.C.'s first official day as a farmer. I made eggs, hash browns, and toast, with coffee and orange juice. The food turned out great. After we were done eating, we couldn't move. We were both so stuffed from breakfast, that when we finally decided to get up, it felt like an hour had gone by.

With breakfast done and out of the way, I gave K.C. a tour of the farm. I showed her where each animal lived and introduced them to her. She was a little nervous around the dogs. Once she got to know them better, she would learn that they would be her knights in shining armor.

Next door to the dogs were the calves. That part she enjoyed. All their little faces made her warm up inside, I could tell. K.C. made that high-pitched ahhh noise that most women make around cute little things.

We made our way to the cheetah area. I told her we wouldn't go in yet. I just wanted her to get a closer look at the cheetah with nobody around and get an idea of what the area looked like. She may have to feed the cheetah sometime. We both stood at the fence and the cheetah sat under the tree near his trough. I couldn't believe that was all he did. Something had to motivate this cheetah to move.

"So, is that like all he does?" K.C. asked.

"I guess so. He moves his head when I feed him, but other than that he just sits in that one spot." I replied. I scratched my head, trying to come up with a real good explanation for all of this, but nothing came from it. As the day went on, I had K.C. do some minor chores. I figured I would give her some easy work to do so that she would be able to take care of it all by herself. I tried not to overwhelm her because there is a lot to do on a farm and all the work takes up most of one's life to keep doing it day after day after day. She seemed happy and pleased to do the easy chores for now.

Two weeks went by before I decided to add a little more to her list. K.C. now had a grip on her normal duties, and it was time for her to learn more. I thought I would show her how to milk a cow.

Cows get milked twice a day. It's something a dairy farmer does a lot. I have a machine that milks the cows to save time. All I did was hook up the machine's nozzles, one for each teat to the cows' udders. The nozzles sucked out the milk. It was very useful on the farm. We milked the cows before we sent them out to graze and again when they came in for the evening.

After I milked two cows, I let K.C. try it. On her first cow, she struggled a bit. The cow got jittery. I wasn't sure if it was the fact it was used to a man's touch instead of a woman's. It took K.C. awhile to get used to milking a cow. She became confident on the last one and was so excited that she wanted to milk another one, but all the cows were out grazing in the field. It reminded me of a time I played golf once. I was doing horrible on the front nine that my back nine was really good. At the end I wanted to play another 18. I guess we get caught up in a moment that doesn't start off good, but when it does, we don't want it to stop.

One day, I tried to let her do her chores all by herself. All I did was ask her if she finished, or how this or that chore went. Occasionally, she needed help, but she was doing a great job. While K.C. did her chores, I checked the stock of food items for the animals. I also looked to see if we needed any food for the house. And I took care of the cheetah. I really wasn't sure if K.C. could handle that kind of pressure yet.

Later that month, K.C. started to ask about the cheetah. "So, when do I help out with the cheetah?"

"I'm not sure you're ready for that yet," I said

"I think I'm ready to try. Can you just give me a chance?"

I thought about it for a while, and then said, "I guess I can, but if it gets too hectic for you or the pressure is too much, you let me know."

"You got it, Captain." she said playfully.

I had a little smile on my face. We would work with the cheetah tomorrow.

The following morning, we got up and ran through our farm routine fairly quickly. In the afternoon, I showed her where the food was. We also took time to look on the cameras to see where the cheetah was and what the rest of the area looked like. I pointed out where the trough was. I grabbed a rifle and some tranquilizer darts, in case I had to use more than one. We got the cheetah food and headed outside.

The cheetah was still in that spot under the tree. I couldn't figure it out. Maybe he was a dumb animal. We got to the front door of the caged area. My heart started to beat a little harder than normal and I had the butterflies in my stomach. I could see that K.C. was also starting to get nervous. As she opened the door, I gave a quick pep talk, hoping it would calm her down.

"Now, I'll have the rifle pointed at him at all times. If he makes a move, I'll tell you. All you have to do is go to the trough over there, put the food in it, and come back here, okay? I'm right here for you and I'll be watching him. This is it. Are you ready?"

"Okay. I can do this," she said in a quiver as if she were in cold water. She turned and headed toward the trough. I had my gun pointed at the cheetah. When the cheetah noticed her, K. C. stopped immediately, but the cheetah didn't make a move. I encouraged K.C., telling her she was doing very well and to just keep going. K.C. moved like she was in a wedding. One-foot-at-a-time toward the trough. About every four steps, she stopped and looked to see where the cheetah was. I reminded her not to panic and I would warn her if the cheetah did anything.

When she got to the trough, she opened the bags of food and put the food in. She turned her head toward the cheetah. I could see that she was breathing very heavily. It must have felt like her heart was trying to pound out of her body.

K.C. made a quick dash. I slowly began to register what happened next. The cheetah got up from his original position and darted after K.C. My heart was thudding back and forth in my body. I had the rifle aimed and was ready to pull the trigger, when I noticed the cheetah decreased his speed and stopped at the trough to eat. I released my finger from the trigger and lowered my rifle from its ready to fire position. K.C. got to the door alright and we both opened it up. I grabbed one of the sleeves of my shirt and wiped all the sweat from my face. K.C. fell to the ground, exhausted. I stood the rifle next to the cage and sat down next to her.

All out of breath she said to me, "You thought I couldn't handle all that?"

"I was only trying to be protective and responsible for your safety." I panted in response.

"So when do we feed him again?" She asked catching some of her breath.

"Around 5:00 p.m."

"Good. See you then." She responded and added with a smirk on her face "*Gramps.*" *Whoa*, I thought. That was an awfully low blow I didn't see coming.

Over the next few weeks, K.C. got more confident feeding the cheetah. Her exits from the area were a lot slower than the first time. The weird thing was the cheetah ate his food right away every time

K.C. delivered it. When I did it, he wouldn't even budge toward it. I must have caused him a problem, but I didn't understand what it was. Every time I fed the cheetah, I asked K.C. if the food was gone. It was gone, but I never saw the cheetah eating it. For some reason the cheetah has something against males.

Day Six Hundred and Seventy

The day finally came for the female cheetah to arrive. I had help from the Marines again to deliver her, but they didn't stay. The bunnies hid in their little house, the dogs barked as usual, and the calves were startled by the noise. The only thing the cows did was just look at the Marines while chewing on the grass with their "oh what a big deal" look. I came over to meet the caravan led by the General.

"Mr. Ellington, are you still here?" the General said jokingly.

"Oh, if you only knew how to get rid of me, General, there might be other things we could talk about."

"Well, this shouldn't take too long. We're only here to deliver the animal and then check-out. You seem to have everything under control."

"Oh, that sounds easy enough. I also have help with me." I signaled K.C. to come over and I introduced her to the General. "This is my farm helper, Kansas City Jones."

K.C. put her hand out for a handshake. "Howdy, General."

"Hello there. Well now, it is very nice to know someone is helping out Mr. Ellington," replied the General.

"Oh, come on, man," I said. We all had a little chuckle for a moment. As we continued to talk, an announcement came over the radio in the truck.

"All units, attention all units! Target is moving toward destination. I repeat, target moving toward destination. Please be

advised and on alert."

The General heard the announcement and gave a signal to the rest of the caravan. We all moved toward the cheetah area. I noticed the male by his tree again.

"Well, here she comes." the General said. At that point I looked up and noticed a strange phenomenon in the sky. Clouds formed rapidly and changed color at the same time. They came toward the farm and seemed to follow the truck that carried the female cheetah. I was confused and wondered why this was happening.

As the truck turned to come to the entrance, I heard an awful noise that I thought sounded like a bunch of ghosts howling. The sound made me shiver and sent chills up and down my back. I looked around to see where the noise was coming from, but couldn't pinpoint it down to one source. The noise continued as the female cheetah got closer. It was so loud and horrendous, that I had to put my hands over my ears to cover them. When I lifted my head up, I looked around to see if anyone else noticed the noise. I saw everyone moving about as if nothing was happening. The ghostly noise grew louder and louder till it was almost deafening. The General and K.C. noticed me and came over to check on me. I told them I wished the noise would stop because it was very loud.

They both asked, "What noise?"

"The one I'm hearing," I replied loudly.

The truck carrying the female cheetah got into place to release her. The cage door opened and the female cheetah walked out and into the cheetah area. The noise I heard stopped immediately. I was relieved and took my hands off my ears. I explained to the General and K.C. about the moaning, ghostly noise that got louder and louder it seemed. They both looked at me with a confused look as if I was making it up. How could I have been the only one to hear such a noise?

After finishing about the alleged ghost noise, we closed the cheetah area and I let everyone know I was okay now. K.C. and I watched the female cheetah interact with the male. They got together and started to sniff each other. At one point, I believed they had sniffed every part of each other. K.C. and I both laughed. After this introduction, the male went back to his spot under the tree and the female followed. She laid down near the male cheetah in the afternoon shade. The Marine caravan had left and it was time for K.C. and me to get back to tending the farm.

When K.C. and I finished our day, we went into the house. K.C. headed for bed, but I stayed up a while to watch the monitors. The main reason I stayed up was that noise I heard earlier. It seemed to bounce around inside my head for a long time, and it never stopped. At one point I thought it came back. I went outside to see if it was real. I peered over my porch to listen for the noise. It came back! This time I needed to know where it was coming from. I made sure to listen carefully to the noise so I could find it right away. I followed in the direction of the barn passing the calves, dogs, and bunnies. The noise wasn't coming from them, but it seemed to be getting louder as I approached the barn. When I got to the door, I was certain it was coming from inside. In all my life I have never been aware of this noise before. I went in and saw that the ghostly noise was coming from the cows. I was amazed that an animal could even come up with a sound like that. I wasn't sure what I could do to make the cows stop. I figured that eventually they will have to stop on their own. I went to bed and heard that sound all through the night. It was then I knew I wasn't going to get much sleep.

During the night or morning, I got up from hearing the noise and went to go watch the cheetahs sleep together under the tree. While I was at the monitors, thoughts started to enter my head. This happened a lot to me and I have come to notice that it happens to people who are alone. My thoughts took me to a time I remembered seeing couples walk hand-in-hand at the store; others sit on a nice patio, or even some at movie theatres with their heads touching. As these thoughts passed through my head, it was a feeling of sorrow that touched me. I have never felt love the way those people experienced it. Tears filled my eyes as I continued to watch the two cheetahs.

A couple days later in the morning, K.C. came up from her room and looked like she'd seen a ghost. I asked her if everything was all right. Breathing heavily, she told me she had a dream and it freaked her out, "In the dream, I was on the farm. It was a beautiful day with the sun shining. The wind blew gently and everything was just the way you wanted it. I walked toward the calf area to feed and pet them. As I did this, the calves and the little houses disappeared. All that was left was an area full of flowers. There were small ones, tall ones, blue ones, green ones, yellow ones and all sorts of other colors, too. I couldn't believe how beautiful it looked. Then I looked into the sky and noticed the clouds were rolling through quickly. They took on the figure of a cheetah that frightened me. I screamed in the dream as loud as I could, but no noise came out. I thought I lost my voice. The cheetah hovered over me, near the flowers, and started to zap them with lightning. When one flower got zapped, it burned up quickly and became a black plant. The lightning moved to another flower, and then another, zapping each one in sight. I couldn't believe my eyes. When it finished, all that was left was me in a field of flowers burnt to a crisp. My eyes filled with tears as I looked back at the cloud. The eyes inside the cloud sent lightning down on me and I screamed as loud as I could again, but there was still no sound."

I tried to calm her down and told her it was only a dream. She was shaking and looked a little disoriented. I put my arms around her and reassured her that nothing was going to happen to her on the farm while I was there. It was just a nightmare.

After breakfast, I gave K.C. an easy day of work on the farm. The dream seemed to suck the life out of her. I was concerned she wasn't going to be able focus much on the farm today.

She seemed to get better as she took care of the rabbits and the dogs.

"Are you feeling any better?"

"I think I'm alright. That dream just took a lot out of me."

"I'll feed the cheetahs today. You can try to relax and take care of yourself."

"Thanks. That should help me get back to my usual self."

Feeding the two cheetahs went by faster than ever. I guess the mood I was in made time go by really quickly. I was excited that my idea worked. The male cheetah was enjoying his new playmate. I didn't think it would have gone that well so soon. I was just trying to make the cheetah happy, and I guess I accomplished that.

Day One Thousand and Thirty-Eight

It had been a year since the female cheetah came to the farm. I was impressed that everything was all right. K.C. and I were having a really good time doing our farm work. We also were really getting to know each other better. I wasn't sure where our relationship was going but we'd begin hugging on occasion. We never kissed or held hands, which was all right with me. I was 74 and she was very young and had a hard time with relationships. All the animals got along with each other. Even the cheetahs had fun with each other. It was as if we were all living in paradise. Still, the dreams and that awful noise haunted the back of my mind. I tried not to let them get to me. After all, they were just dreams and noises that really didn't mean anything. What harm could they cause the farm?

At one point in time, K.C. and I noticed that the weather on the farm went through some weird changes. The sun never showed itself. Clouds covered the sky all day and all night. The grass changed to a pale yellow in color. I didn't notice it for some time. We should have been more aware when the yellow grass formed around the house and rabbit house too. For most of my life the ground was always green and I should've been more aware of it at the time, but for some reason my mind was on other things. I'd never seen the sky cloudy for a long period of time in my life. I began to wonder, what was happening to the farm?

One day around lunchtime, K.C. came running to me after

I'd just finished filling the cheetah trough. "James, something happened."

"What's wrong?" I asked.

"You have to come see this."

I was worried that something terrible had happened. K.C. led me to the calf area. I noticed the dogs barking at the cheetahs. It took my focus away of what K.C. wanted to show me. I couldn't just let the dogs keep barking. The sound in their bark was almost like an angry growl, which really meant get out of my way. I ran over to them and tried to calm them down by petting them and talking to them softly, reassuring them everything was fine. They wouldn't stop barking for a while.

It was a little later that the dogs finally calmed down and stopped barking. I went back to the calves and where K.C. was. I started to sense a feeling of fear or uneasiness as I got closer. For some reason, all the calves were in their little houses. The only time the calves would be there was to sleep or get out of the rain. It was cloudy outside, but not raining, and it wasn't time for them to go to sleep. I was confused.

K.C. stood at the middle-most calf house. She told me she was feeding the calves when she noticed all of them were inside their houses. She added that she could hear their chains rattling. I had her pause for a little bit to see if I could hear it to. Sure enough, the chains were rattling. I looked around but it was too dark to see anything in the calf houses.

I went to the house to get a flashlight. I came back and checked each house. When I looked into a house, I turned the flashlight on to see where each calf was. I pointed the light where my foot was and then slowly moved the light around the four-walled house.

I was trying not to scare the calves so I made sure not to put the light directly in their eyes. When I saw the calf, it was shaking violently. I had never seen the calves do that before. Okay, maybe when I checked on them during a storm, but that was the only time I saw them shake like that.

I moved on to the next house and saw the same thing. All the calves were shaking violently. I came back to the first house, were K.C. was still standing. I told her the rattle was the calves shaking because they were scared of something.

"Well, that doesn't surprise me," she said. "Wait till you see this."

She pointed to the chain of a calf house. The calf houses were taller versions of a dog house; five feet tall and about as long as a king-sized bed. Almost like a little shack. Inside was some straw on the ground to make it comfortable for the calf. On the outside of the house, near the opening, was a chain latch to keep the calf close so it couldn't wander off. A crate hung on the side wall near the opening and along with the chain latch. In the crate was hay for the calf. Adjacent to the crate on the other side was a bottle of water held by a bottle-holder. The bottles were big. At the end of each one was a rubber piece that let a little bit of water out when you squeezed it.

I looked at the chain and noticed that it wasn't rattling. I became nervous, uncertain what to do next.

"Grab the chain and pull it," K.C. said.

I got a hold of the chain and was hoping it would pull back, but it didn't.

"Pull it," K.C. shouted.

I looked at her like *who are you to yell at me?* I didn't say anything, but let the anger in my body start to stir a little bit, and took it out on pulling the chain. With both hands, I yanked the chain out. It really wasn't hard. I thought it might be, because the way the other calves were frightened, they probably didn't want to come out. As the chain came to the end, I knew why it didn't take much effort. At the end was a collar, and it was unbuckled.

I dropped to my knees. Tears started to fill my eyes. I could not believe one of my calves was gone. For a long moment, I was on my knees crying for my missing calf. The only thing K.C. could do was comfort me. I heard her sniffling as well, but I couldn't see her. I was too busy looking at the empty collar, crying.

After a while, I got up from the empty shack and started a search for the missing calf. I had K.C. look in one of the barns and around the cheetah area while I searched the field where the cows are. I took my tractor to save time and speed up my search. I couldn't afford to waste any time. If the calf got out, we could possibly catch it before anything happened to it.

A couple hours had passed and we came back to the calf area with nothing. What could've happened to the calf? I tried to think, but I was too worried to form any kind of logic in my mind that made any sense. The only thing I could do was hope for the best and prepare for the worst.

We left and went inside the house. I called the police to report a stolen calf. The officer on the other end didn't seem like he was in the mood to deal with my missing calf. I also checked to see if there had been any car accidents within the Cowlic area before I hung up. I didn't get a response to either item. At this point, I knew the police were not going to help me.

So I called Ted, the neighbor who I trade milk for feed with. I asked him if he'd seen Mawdy. I named the calf Mawdy because when she was born, she mooed a lot. Ted said that he hadn't seen or heard anything, but he would let me know if something came up. I told him I appreciated it, and asked if he could have all the other neighbors keep a look-out. He said he was sorry that this happened to me. I thanked him and hung up. It was nice to know someone out there would help me.

I didn't feel like doing much of anything the rest of the day, but I had to. That was the one thing about being a farmer I really didn't like. You never got any days off.

A couple of days went by without any word of Mawdy. K.C. tried to see if someone she knew had any information that could help us. She told him what had happened, and asked him to watch out for any information on Mawdy. It was all K.C. could do.

I still made some calls around the neighborhood trying anything to get my calf back alive at any cost. I had a couple of people respond telling me that they were told that some dangerous animals were spotted among the community. Some neighbors heard that a mountain lion was spotted several miles to the east of Cowlic. A couple of others heard a coyote was spotted north of our area. No one heard of any missing calf or finding a calf dead or alive for that matter. I am sure that if a mountain lion or coyote came by I would have known about it. There was still hope in my mind, though if the calf was wondering it may have come across a rattler. I would have hated to have thought that.

The next night, I received a call back from Ted.

"Hey James, I think I saw one of your calves lurking in my cornfield. I really never got a good look at the creature, but it might just be your missing calf." Ted said.

I felt a little bit of hope fill my body. I told him, "I will be over to help you search your field to make sure it is there." I got myself over to Ted's farm as quickly as I could. Ted was waiting for me. He had blue jeans on, a blue flannel shirt under a brown leathery type coat most cowboys wore. He also had boots and a cowboy hat as well. When I saw Ted, he reminded me of Dennis Quaid. He was leaning on his giant red truck. The one that has the motor really loud and it sounds like a train when it drives.

"Ready to do this," Ted said.

"Ready whenever you are," I replied. We got into the truck and drove to his corn field. We came to the opening of the field and got out. Ted brought two flashlights out and gave one to me. We turned on the flashlights and started to search for the wandering animal. While we were walking, we were moving our flashlights side to side not to miss anything in front of us. I must admit I was a little freaked out by searching for an animal at night in a corn field, because the animal could jump out of nowhere and scare the bones out of you. I don't like being scared. Suddenly we both heard a rustling sound among the corn stalks. It sounded like the noise came from up ahead of us. We both decided to quicken our pace now. Ted was a couple rows to my left. We continued moving forward and what felt like closer to the sound.

At one point I heard Ted say, "There you are" to the creature. Before Ted made another move the creature ran across the stalks and stopped in my row of the field. I wasn't sure what it was, but it had stopped five yards ahead of me. I got my flashlight pointed in front of me and continued walking slowly not to alert the creature. As I got closer I noticed that there were what appeared to be two yellow dots in the distance. I raised my flashlight to shine the light on what was in the darkness. The light revealed the creature as a sheep. The little sheep baaa'd at us and continued to eat part of the corn stalks. I, however, was not happy and still mad at the fact that Mawdy was still missing.

The following night, I walked into the house with my mouth wide open. As I fell onto my comfy recliner staring up at the ceiling in the living room, K.C. came and asked if everything was okay.

"No, it's not." I was upset.

"What happened?" she asked. "I noticed you were out there for a while."

"Yep. Let me tell you why." I was now a little more than upset.

"Okay." K.C. had a quiet voice, as if she was scared of what was coming next.

"K.C., please forgive me. I am not mad at you. I'm sorry if it seems that way. But tonight, as I brought the cows into the barn, something happened."

K.C. knelt to the floor by my feet. She was in a pink robe and her hair was in a ponytail that went straight down her back.

"As I was bringing the cows in the barn to be milked, I noticed they were uneasy. They were all piled up at the door. I tried to get them in as calmly as I could. Then I noticed one cow was missing."

It was a Jersey cow named Sue. Sue had been on the farm for a long time. She and I were like best pals. She seemed like the alpha female of the group and took charge of everything that happened in the field when I wasn't around. Sue was the first cow in the barn and the last cow out to the field. I would usually give her a little chit-chat before excusing her to her duties as cow leader.

"Oh, my word," she gasped.

"I called for Sue, and I even whistled for a minute. When Sue didn't respond, I got into my tractor and went to search for her. I looked all around but never spotted the cow. I have no idea why cows are disappearing from the farm, but something isn't right. What am I supposed to do?"

"I'm not sure there is anything more we can do. We've got people watching if something comes up. Right now, all we can do is to try not to think about it and move on."

I couldn't do that. That was hoping for things to get better when they seemed to be getting worse. It just doesn't work that way.

I went to bed but I didn't get much sleep. All night, I heard that ghostly noise coming from the barn. It was so annoying. For some reason, the cows seemed to mourn the loss of Sue.

The next day, I looked to see where the cheetahs were. At this point, I couldn't rule anything out. I hoped that they were in a different spot, but they weren't. They were both lying down in the shade under that tree. That was still puzzling to me. There was no logical reason a cheetah would choose to live under a tree or stay there for a long period of time. I guess finding out where the cheetahs were this whole time ruled them out of being a possible threat or reason the cows were disappearing. I double checked the cage door to see if it had been left open or broken down. It looked like it was still brand new and never used before. I walked around the caged area as well just to see if I had missed anything. Not a single sign pointed out that the cheetah did it. My investigation to see who or what was responsible for the missing cows revealed nothing. I thought of every possibility that I could think of and all I came up with was that it was time for K.C. to head back to the newspaper office to see what she could dig up.

Day One Thousand and Forty-Seven

The President made a deal with K.C. that she could help me on the farm and take a sabbatical from the newspaper. She was able to return to the paper whenever she wanted. I told K.C. that I needed her help at the newspaper office to see if she could find any information on the missing cows. It was the only thing I could think of that could possibly help us figure out what happened. I needed to make sure we covered every possible end to this mystery, and knowing her friends in the news industry, something was bound to come her way. She didn't think this was necessary, but she said she would do it for my sake. K.C. got her things together and, three days later, returned to her real job. Now, the only thing left to do was to wait and hope something happened. Nothing did.

My search continued with K.C.'s help. After K.C. got back into town to do some research on our missing animals, I decided I would call her about three days later to see what she had come up with.

"Did you find anything out?" I asked.

"I really haven't found any information out yet. I am sorry. I am hoping something turns up."

"I thought if I gave you some time something was bound to stir up. You tried your best and that is all I would expect from anyone. Would you let me know if something comes up? I really would appreciate it."

"Okay, and James, I am truly sorry this happened to you. Take care."

"I know Kansas City. You take care of yourself" I hung up.

I stood looking out the kitchen window one rainy day, trying to think. All I got was a blank. It was the blank of wanting to figure out an answer but getting lost in a trance and forgetting the original problem.

After another year went by, all the animals disappeared except for the dogs. I just couldn't understand where they went or what happened to them. It was like they never existed at all. I know that sounds kind of weird, but that was how it felt. It still bothered me that I couldn't figure it out. I asked everyone I knew if they saw or heard anything.

Everyone I contacted responded the same way. "No, I haven't seen any of them. Yes, we are doing our best to find them."

I wasn't certain what my next step was. As a farmer, the animals were my life. Now that they weren't here, I was completely lost. My life seemed to have taken a turn for the worse. It seemed hopeless.

Could I buy more cows? Where would I get the money? Who would help me? I thought about asking the President, but that would take months: send him a letter and wait for one back, have a truck deliver a bunch of new cows to get used to, et cetera. At my age, I really didn't want a bunch of new animals. I didn't want to start over. I wasn't sure if I would be able to contact my family. Asking for help never came easy to me. I was always able to handle my own problems and I somehow got through without much help from anyone. I couldn't bother my family that lives all over the U.S. It was pretty clear to me that I couldn't afford any new cows or animals.

Next, I thought about getting a new job. I chuckled at the idea of a seventy-six year old man looking for a job. Who would want a person who farmed all his life? What job could I really do? Nope, that wasn't going to work either.

I tried to make do with what was left of my farming life. It may have been way past its time, but I decided to hang out with the dogs more. It seemed like a good idea especially now, since all the other animals were gone and the dogs were acting a little weird. They were always looking for my attention. I was now able to give it to them more freely. That lasted a couple of days, but I was not sure I could keep up the same routine.

I did know that there was something that bothered me about the dogs, though. When I wasn't around, I noticed they would sit beside their houses and look toward the cheetah area whimpering. They were always doing that. When I came out to play with them, they turned their attention toward me and played with me. But when I left, they returned to their original positions and whimpered. The thing that really worried me was whenever it rained or snowed, they were outside their houses. I decided that I would have my veterinarian make a house-call, or in this case, a farm-call, to check on the dogs.

When the veterinarian came to the farm, I explained what was going on. He was the same veterinarian who came to check on all the animals. He always showed up in that white coat that gave me the willies. He was tall and thin with blond hair and a northern Canadian accent; your typical doctor who all the ladies swooned over when he would check on them. He told me I shouldn't worry about the dogs much, but he went over to check on them just in case.

When he got to the dogs, they did the same thing. They noticed the vet and focused their attention on him. The dogs were very good around people and always looked for attention. I waited for the veterinarian to finish and come back to the house.

"Well, ya know James? They both seem as healthy as the winner of the Westminster. I'm not sure why they're acting this way. So, I guess there's no need for alarm."

"Are you sure they're okay? They don't seem like it. They seem sad to me."

"Hey," he said. "I am only an animal doctor. What do I know?"

"Sorry, but something doesn't seem right. Anyway, what's the damage?"

"I'm supposed to send the bill to the government now, okay? I understand your concern now that they are your only two animals left. Just try to take it easy now James, and don't get too over-worked about the dogs. This may be a phase."

When the veterinarian left, I went back to the porch to watch the dogs. They would not move, even when a butterfly fluttered right in front of them. Something really got to them. I didn't think that it was a phase, but I wasn't the veterinarian. I decided to go back to the house and see if something needed to be worked on in the workshop.

I made a little stop on my way to where K.C. used to bunk. The little den area was vacant and it seemed kind of purposeless for being a room. I found an album book on the desk I had put in for K.C. I forgot that K.C. had a camera and took pictures of the animals, her, the farm, and me. I paged through it taking notice of the way each picture was taken and how she managed to make it look incredible. I was stunned at certain ones on how she captured the scenery. It made me look at the farm in a different perspective.

When I reached the end of the album, there was an envelope. It had been there as if it was waiting for me to find it. I opened it and read the note inside it.

> *Dear James,*
>
> *Well, we certainly had a great time on the farm, didn't we? I want to thank you for letting me be able to help you out with the farm work. Saying good bye isn't easy nor is it hard. It seems to be an awkward word that fills something. I'm not sure that it's meant to fill because once it is said you can only utter it back in response. I want to let you know, that you are a wonderful person and fun to be around. You have certainly showed me a side to someone I have never seen. It was great while it lasted. I hope in the end, everything turns out for you. I want you to have this album to remember all the fun times we had and hopefully there are some pictures in here that make you laugh or even smile. I know I had a blast. Thanks for being a friend!*
>
> *Sincerely,*
>
> *K.C. (Kansas City) Jones*

I closed the album and mashed it up against my face for a while. I was absolutely in awe of the album, the pictures, and all the hard work that K.C. took to makes this. I cried for some time. When I finished, I felt a bolt of lightning strike my head. Was the album a clue? I wasn't sure where to look for the clue, but I could feel my body resonate inside me. I went through the album again paging and looking at each picture. I stopped at a picture K.C. took of one of the cheetahs. It looked very good and was in perfect focus almost like the picture was really in front of you. As I continued to look at the cheetah, I noticed the head moved towards me and started to growl. The next thing that happened was the head opened its mouth and tried to bite my head off.

I dropped the album because it seemed so real to me. When I realized the album was on the floor, a thought struck me as I went to grab it off the floor. The idea of taking pictures with a camera made me remember that we had cameras all around the farm. I could go back in time on the computer to see what happened the night Mawdy went missing. I was relieved but also upset at myself. I should have figured that out at the start. Why couldn't I figure it out? I wondered. That should have been the next place to look at when Mawdy or any other cow disappeared. I put the album back on the table and went straight to the computer.

I sat down at the computer and went back to video footage of the day Mawdy went missing. I set the time of the camera to when I went to bed. I clicked on the camera to view the area overlooking the calves' houses and zoomed in for a closer look. I watched and waited, hoping to notice something that went on while I slept. I wasn't sure what I was looking for, but I needed answers and I needed them now. Then it happened.

I saw the dogs on the left side of the screen start barking. It was 1:05 a.m. As the dogs continued to bark, I noticed a figure move between the calf houses. I couldn't make it out at first. The figure went into one of the houses. You could see the house move a little as a struggle went on inside. The dogs were probably barking at the top of their lungs by this time. The house continued to shake, and then it stopped. I waited to see the creature come out. At 1:30, it came out with the calf in its mouth. I clicked a button to pause the video to get a good look at the creature. In that brief moment, I couldn't believe my eyes…

It was the cheetah!

Day One Thousand Four Hundred Twenty

I couldn't believe it. Where did I go wrong? I sat on the porch, looking around at what now seemed like a ghost town. The barns and little houses were empty, yet filled with silence. The only sound was the rattle of hanging chains against the wind. The farm grass had turned from a bright green color, bursting with life, to a barren mix of dark brown and yellowish straw. The sky remained dark after all the recent events on the farm. The sun no longer shone through the clouds. I've heard that weather changes all the time, but I cannot explain the reasons for this.

All the time the cheetahs were killing my cows, and I never saw it. I felt downcast. They must have been really terrified. I looked over at Taz and Duke. They were both lying on the ground, waiting for me to make a move. I didn't think I would be able to move from the porch after all the shock from figuring out what had been going on. Everything I had was taken from me in what seemed like a flash.

I forced myself up from the porch and went over to the dogs, looking for some comfort. I wasn't sure if I'd find it there, but I was willing to try anything right now. They got excited as I walked over. I could tell by the way they wagged their tails. It was amazing to know how dogs sense what a person is feeling, and are able to respond toward those feelings, like when a person is angry, a dog will help them out by playing with them to get their mind off of being angry. We played for a while, in our own little world. But after that, I felt like there was only one thing left to do.

I stopped playing with the dogs and went into the house. I went to the weapon cabinet, grabbed a rifle and bullets and carried them back out to the porch. There, I loaded the rifle with two bullets and put the rest in my pocket. I unhitched the dogs from their chains. When I unhooked them, they started to run and jump up and down around me. They were in a very playful mood. I patted them and tried to settle them down. They got quiet and seemed to calm down. I looked up toward the one area we had to go, where the cheetahs lived. I had a weird feeling as I looked. I wasn't sure what it was or how to describe it.

I started to walk toward the cheetah area. The dogs noticed my movement and followed right behind me. As we neared the entrance, memories filled my head of the days when both cheetahs came to the farm; how they looked as the trucks brought them in. I remember when the vehicles came and brought all the people from around the country to see the cheetahs. It warmed my heart and I smiled as I touched the door. The door was a shiny gray when I installed it. But now, with time and the weather change, this once gray door was a rusty maroon.

All of this should never have happened to begin with. I should have realized this was not a good idea. What kind of farmer would consider watching a dangerous animal with an abundant supply of live food nearby? Why didn't I tell the President the truth about not helping try to train a wild cheetah? Was I scared, or were the benefits too much to pass up? Whatever the reason, it happened, and it was too late to look back.

I opened the fence door and waited for the dogs to pass through before I followed. Once they were clear of the door, I shut it. I figured that having the dogs with me might give me a better chance of dealing with the cheetahs if I needed them to do so. I wasn't sure I would be able to kill the cheetah in the first place. I have never fired a gun in my life.

I'd never paid attention to the vastness of this area before. Most of my time was spent watching pictures of it on the computer monitors in the control room. It was a blur when I rushed in and out to deliver the food. But this was a new look for me. I walked up one of the small hills. Once I reached the top, I got a really good view of the land. I tried to take in as much as I could. The straw-like grass covered the dusty ground. What stood out in my mind was that it hadn't rained much since the female cheetah came. I was not sure why.

It didn't take long for me to get back to reality. As I got close to where I thought the cheetahs lived, I felt my heart pounding harder with each step. I wish I could tell you I was brave, but I was not. I was scared. I had no clue what was going to happen.

With no sight of the cheetahs, I figured I would double check to see if my rifle was loaded. I always like to check things twice and I remember in a movie that the protagonist checked his gun to make sure it was loaded properly before going off to kill the bad guys. Better safe than sorry I used to tell myself. I opened up the barrel to see if there was any ammo in it. Check. It was loaded. I clicked the barrel back into place.

Lightning flashed across the sky, followed shortly by a crash of thunder. During the lighting flash, I noticed a dark figure with orange eyes standing twenty feet away. I had seen those eyes before. More thunder was followed by another flash of lightning. The second flash made it clear what the dark figure was. It was the male cheetah! My blood started to boil, my heart raced faster and I was filled with more rage than ever before.

I let my emotions get the best of me and yelled out, "It is all your fault!" My stress level went up. I started to breathe very deeply.

"Who do you think you are? I gave you land to live on and food to eat. I, yes I, even got you another cheetah. I thought you needed company. But no thanks were given. Not a single word whatsoever. And then, you killed all my cows!" I stopped. I noticed another dark figure joining the male cheetah. It was the female. She walked up and lay her body down next to him. Taz and Duke were upright on the ground next to me, sensing danger.

"What do you have to say for yourself?" I looked down at the ground and chuckled at the absurdity of this last question. Sometimes, I am a fool with words.

The next thing I heard was, "You humans are so pathetic."

I looked up from chuckling and stared at the cheetahs, puzzled and confused. "Who said that?" I looked around to see if there was someone else around trying to be funny.

The voice answered again, "You humans are so pathetic!"

The voice seemed to come from one of the cheetahs. I had to be certain. "I'm sorry, what was that again?" I focused on both of the cheetahs.

"He said that humans are pathetic." This time the female answered.

"What do you mean, humans are pathetic?"

Now the male cheetah spoke. "You humans will do anything and everything to get free money or anything free for that matter."

My jaw dropped in shock. The cheetahs were communicating telepathically. How was this happening?

"Your question has already been answered since it is now a reality to you."

"What gives you the right to call humans pathetic?" I asked.

"It seems you and the rest of the humans are not the brightest species. Look at the ant: The ant works hard with other ants to build a home and collect food. The smallest creature trusts its own kind, whereas humans need a motivational tool to get a job done. It's kind of pointless. Would any human do anything without getting something in return?"

"We need money to be able to purchase things. How else could we live?"

"It would take a miracle for humans to rely on each other and work together."

"How can you say that?" I asked. "You don't know what we're capable of."

"I have been all over the place. I traveled from Africa to Europe by plane, and then on to America, by boat. In Africa, man treated everything as if it had value and importance; food, water, clothing, medicine, time, work, school, people, and the list goes on and on. It seemed like everywhere else I went; humans did anything they could to get money. They bought lottery tickets, gambled, manipulated, robbed, and even used publicity to get more money. It was quite a sight watching their eyes light up for something they expected, only to blow it on stuff they didn't need. I first saw this happen on a boat. A couple of crewmen were rolling dice. They played a game where they bet money based on the outcome of the dice. The winner got all the money placed down before each roll. It seemed like a terrible way to lose money. Only one person benefited. I have also heard of people who got robbed in the night.

Still, only one person benefited. It is always about one person; one person to be on top, one person to rule over the others. It is sad."

I couldn't believe what I was hearing. Humans are pathetic? They only do things to benefit themselves? I wasn't looking for a lecture. "What does this have to do with me?"

"I am glad you asked," the male cheetah replied. "Aren't you a human?"

"I am, but I have never benefited off of anyone else. "

"Aren't you a farmer?"

"Yes. What does that have to with anything?"

"You grow crops, provide milk and other items to benefit others. Right?"

"Yes, that's how I make a living. It is all about helping others out. Other parts of the world don't have farmlands and can't grow crops or provide common goods. So farmers like me, who have land, help out those areas that don't."

"Oh... that is a good point, but aren't you doing that to get money. You did think about that, right? We animals work together and are able to accomplish things together. We have to rely on each other; otherwise we become detached and make a mess of the way of life. I really don't see how animals and humans are alike."

"Well, not all of us are out to benefit ourselves over the other. Now that I know you can talk, I...was... wondering..." I started to stumble over my words. I had almost forgotten that I was in the presence of two dangerous animals.

Also, I noticed a strong odor in the air. It smelled worse than a case of rotten eggs. *God, what is that awful smell?* I covered my nose and mouth with a handkerchief, hoping to make the smell less potent, but it didn't help much. The wind kept the smell swirling around us. I couldn't take it much longer. With a muffled voice I asked the cheetahs. "What happened to the cows?"

In a sarcastic tone the male cheetah looked at me and said, "What do you think that smell is?"

"What do you mean?"

"Take a look over that hill." The hill to my left led to a kettle formed in the land. It was big and very deep. You couldn't see inside the kettle from where the cameras were positioned. There was a steamy cloud coming from the kettle, like it was full of boiling water. The steam carried the strong smell and my eyes started to water. I walked over to get a look at what was in the kettle. The dogs followed so they could be close and not to lose sight of me. Through the cloud, I saw decaying cow bodies in one big pile. Cow bones and carcasses were lying on top of one another in the kettle.

I stood there speechless. I noticed little cow bones were in the pile too. The calves were eaten as well as the adults. Hatred filled every area of my body. All my hard work on this farm was taken away from me. And for what? To satisfy an animal's hunger? I walked back to where I was before with the dogs following and glared at the cheetahs. "Why?"

The cheetahs looked at each other and then back at me without saying a single word.

This time I yelled. "Why!"

"Why, *what?*" the male asked.

"Why did you kill my cows?"

"They were very useful to us. The meat you were serving was fine for a little bit. But we needed to chase, attack, and enjoy the hunt for real food. Life in Africa was better; an open area not constricted by a fence, with easy access to food and water. Here, we had to wait on you and that girl to provide. I almost fell over in exhaustion from how slow you both moved."

"My cows were not meant for your leisure. They were a means to earn money and produce milk. You took that away from me."

"I have no sympathy for your lack of judgment. You should've realized what bringing a wild and dangerous animal to your farm would result in, let alone two. You're pathetic."

"I thought that bringing another animal would make you happy."

"Oh, so the cheetah all alone needs a friend to play with. 'We felt sorry for the poor *whittle* cheetah because he was all *a-wone.* Grow up!'" The male mimicked in a child voice. "And you *think?* You think? I am sorry, but since when does a wild animal need a human to think for it? Did I have a sign on my forehead saying, "Need a friend to play with?" I think not. As for killing your precious cows, you obviously forgot the fact that nature will run its course."

This added more fuel to the fire. I tried to control my feelings before something happened that was out of my control. I was just a guy who tried to help out one of God's creatures. I felt a little thank you was in order, but I didn't expect the cheetah would see it my way. Apparently, he was more concerned with how humans treated him. There was no remorse from him or his companion.

Now, the clouds were growing darker and darker. Lightning flashed several times. I tried to stay calm and reasonable, but all I really wanted to do was aim my rifle at the cheetah and blow him into oblivion. My rage and anger grew more intense. My heart pumped so hard that it felt like it was going to burst out of my body.

"So, this is how it ends."

The male cheetah responded with, "There's only one who knows how things end. All I can say is, whatever happens, happens for a reason."

Was he talking about God and Spirituality? Did he know who God was? The male cheetah was so arrogant. I yelled at the cheetah the one thing I wanted to know. "Did you know what you did was wrong? Do you feel guilty for stealing something that wasn't yours? Are you sorry?"

After yelling, I paused to gather myself from the buildup of anger. The male cheetah turned to look at the female, and then back at me. "How can I be sorry for natural instinct?"

"Well, I cannot control what happens next."

The cheetah replied, "So be it."

This conversation made me angrier the longer it went on. Something had to stop it. A flash of lightning came, followed by another roar of thunder. I tried to calm myself down, but as I looked at the cheetah, my hatred intensified. The cheetahs killed my cows. Now I wanted to repay the favor by killing the cheetahs.

I came up with a plan to kill them. I am not sure I even liked it, but it seemed worth a shot. My plan was to send the dogs to attack the cheetahs. I've seen it done on TV and in movies, but I have never sent an animal to attack another before.

Both dogs rose from their seated positions as if they knew something was about to happen. I looked down at Taz, and then Duke. Both stared straight back at me. They knew it was time for them to get ready to attack. Animals are still fascinating to me sometimes. They knew when something was going to happen, and when something was wrong. I waited a minute or two before sending the dogs off. There was a chance that the dogs may not return.

I knelt down and patted them on the head, as if I was saying goodbye. I got back to my feet and pointed at the two cheetahs.

That's when I yelled, "Attack."

The dogs growled and charged the cheetahs. I noticed as the dogs got closer, the cheetahs kept still. With the dogs about 10 yards away, I thought surely the cheetahs would move. Nope. Not a single muscle flinched. When the dogs were within two yards, the cheetahs stood their ground. I figured out why.

A third and fourth cheetah came flying over the original two and crashed into the dogs. The cheetahs pounced, slamming the dogs into the ground. Both sets of animals got back up and attacked each other. The fight consisted of a lot of growling, biting, clawing, bleeding, and roaring. All I could do was stand there, shocked and amazed. I wasn't sure where these cheetahs came from. They looked almost like the adults but not full grown. I thought the government was supposed to make sure that the original cheetahs couldn't have babies. That topic would have to be dealt with later.

The fight kept on going and because of the lack of rain, the animals kicked up a big cloud of dust from the ground. It was hard to see what was going on. I could only hear the sounds of the battle.

Suddenly the noises stopped. I waited for the dust cloud to dissipate. When my eyes adjusted, the images surrounded by the cloud came into focus. My two dogs lay on the ground, breathless and still. Tears streamed from my eyes as the emptiness of loss entered my soul. Memories flashed through my head, from when I first got them, to the moment we left the front porch. My favorite playmates on the farm were gone.

My face and body overflowed with rage. I wanted to scream out loud. Clenching my teeth as hard as I could, I aimed the rifle at the adult cheetahs. They were still in their same spot. I was about to pull the trigger, but I stopped. I stopped because I noticed something missing that was there a moment ago; some *things*. The two new cheetahs were gone.

Where did they go? I looked around but couldn't find them. My face quickly shifted from anger to confusion. I scanned the area again for the new cheetahs, but they were gone. Maybe they ran away somewhere together; maybe they vanished into thin air. All I knew was they were here and then they weren't.

I lifted my rifle and aimed a third time. As I got my finger ready to pull the trigger, my eye caught a glimpse of a dark figure to my right. It was the third cheetah. It moved so quickly, I hadn't realized where it went. As my eyes came back to the adults I looked over to the left and spotted the fourth. They were on either side of me, ready to strike. *Clever beasts!*

I still had the rifle pointed at the adults. My heart pounded rapidly. *It was now or never.* I looked at the male cheetah and noticed him blink his eye. The way he blinked his eye appeared like a delayed reaction. Normally a blink lasts a second. The male cheetah's blink took a couple of seconds. When he finished, I heard a growl from both of the new cheetahs. I was taken aback by the simultaneous growl. They started to walk toward me, and their pace quickened to a full charge. Their quickness really caught me off guard. I didn't have time to stop them with my rifle.

The two charging cheetahs crashed into me and started biting, and hurting me. I tried to defend myself as best I could, but the cheetahs were too much for me. Splashes of red surrounded my body and the cheetahs. I tried to crawl away, but they pulled me back. They dragged me back to the tree and I saw all four cheetahs around me.

Then it happened. I could hear the crunching of mouths around me. My body was being torn apart. I screamed in agony. I couldn't believe that I was still alive while they ate me. Was it possible? I began to see a white light and within it I saw myself being born in the hospital, my parents both happy at what they accomplished. Moments of my childhood went by, with visions of my family. The recent events with the government, the cheetahs and K.C. came next.

As I lay there on the ground in a pool of my own blood, I wondered if I could have changed anything. Could I have done anything differently? These thoughts ran through my head until I realized I couldn't change the past. I had choices to make, and I made them.

Epilogue

As time went on, the government didn't know what to about the cheetahs. They gave K.C. the choice of what should happen to them. She chose to have the cheetahs taken to a wildlife area where they could live the rest of their days. The farm and house rotted and withered with the changing seasons and passage of time. The ground became desolate and unsuitable for food and crops. It turned into a memory for those who came and encountered the farm and all that was in it. Neighbors treated it as a memorial to me, and paid their respect until they too joined the great farm in the sky. My time on the farm wasn't great, nor was it terrible. I lived my life to the fullest. I have always heard that everything happens for a reason. That saying boggled my mind and I was uncertain of its meaning. But now I have a clearer understanding.

Afterword

It all started in sophomore English class. The teacher gave the class an assignment to write a one-page story. One boy thought long and hard on what he could come up with for a story. He came back the next day with a story worthy of a good grade. The cover was the way he wanted it and he handed it in.

A couple days later, he received his story with a grade on it. One of the other students noticed its cover and rushed over to see what it was. He asked if he could read the boy's story. The boy a little puzzled and bewildered at why someone would want the story agreed and gave it to him. About a day later, it became a big hit among their group of friends.

Two months later, the boy and the other student were working on a project for the same class. The student still had his face in the one-page story, and it was becoming a distraction. The boy told the other student, several times, to get to work on the project instead of reading the story. The student paid no attention, and continued to enjoy the one-page story. The boy got up, took the story, ripped it up in front of the student, and placed it in the blue recycling bin. The story was gone, for what some might have thought of as *forever*. The boy went on and forgot about stories and books.

Until one Christmas, seven years after the story was destroyed, the boy received a gift that would spark a fire to write a novel inspired by the original story. The gift was a book from the boy's brother. The boy remembered his love for books and found the motivation to write the story all over. And now, here is the story that took several years to become a reality.

Michael Young

Living with a Cheetah... or More